OCEAN PRIZE

When a valuable cargo ship is abandoned in mid-Atlantic Captain Barling of the *s.s. Hopeful Enterprise* has very special reasons for wishing to tow it into port. The question is is he justified in risking men's lives for the sake of his own desires?

Adam Loder, mate of the *Hopeful Enterprise*, thinks it is nothing but a wild goose chase anyway; and Jonah Madden, the chief engineer, is worried about his ailing engines. But Charlie Wilson has a deeper worry. He has killed a woman in Montreal and fears that the police will pick him up on arrival in England. That is why he volunteers for the riskiest job of all.

It is not only the sea that threatens Barling's chances of success—though that is bad enough in the autumn gales—there is also a very tenacious rival to contend with in the shape of a salvage tug with a tough and not over-scrupulous crew.

OCEAN PRIZE

James Pattinson

ROBERT HALE · LONDON

ISBN-10: 0-7090-8057-3
ISBN-13: 978-0-7090-8057-2

Robert Hale Limited
Clerkenwell House
Clerkenwell Green
London EC1R 0HT

2 4 6 8 10 9 7 5 3 1

Printed in Great Britain by
St Edmundsbury Press Limited, Bury St Edmunds, Suffolk.
Bound by Woolnough Bookbinding Limited.

CONTENTS

ONE

LAST VOYAGE

CAPTAIN BARLING stood on the bridge of the S.S. *Hopeful Enterprise* and watched the wheat dripping into number two hold. The huge grain silos overshadowed the Montreal wharf and dwarfed the vessel as she lay there taking her cargo, motionless, silent, her engines stopped, settling almost imperceptibly deeper and deeper into the water.

It was a fine, rather warm October day and the sun shone down on the grimy steel of decks and bulwarks and glinted on the windows of the wheelhouse. The wheat flowed from the spout suspended over the hold and turned to liquid gold in the bright sunlight. And it was indeed gold, Barling thought; the rich gold of the Canadian prairies; and it seemed scarcely right that it should be pouring into so time-worn and battered a ship.

For the *Hopeful Enterprise* was undoubtedly old. George Barling could remember standing on that same bridge some thirty years ago, watching wheat flow into the holds just as he was watching it now. He had been a young third mate then and there had been guns mounted on the wings of the bridge and on the poop. And the name of the ship had not been *Hopeful Enterprise*; that was the name he and Bruce Calthorp had given her years later; given her in hope and expectation of great things to come; hope that had slowly faded, expectation that had never been fulfilled.

In 1942 Barling had been twenty-four years old and the S.S. *Fort Rock* had been a new ship, a 7,000 ton British standard type, the kind that was being built as fast as the yards could manage in order to replace the immense tonnage that was being lost to U-boat and Nazi bomber. Barling had served in the *Fort Rock* for a year before being transferred to another ship as second mate. It was twenty years later when he and Bruce Calthorp went into partnership and bought her on a fifty-fifty basis and changed the name to *Hopeful Enterprise*.

Calthorp had been full of confidence. " We'll make a go of it, George. With you as master and with me to look after things ashore, we'll really make it work. Ten years from now Barling and Calthorp will be a shipping line to reckon with."

It was by way of being a sentimental as well as a commercial project for Barling; he had not forgotten those early experiences of his in convoy with the *Fort Rock*, and it was with surprise and no little delight that he discovered that she was still afloat. She could so easily have been at the bottom of the Atlantic or the Pacific or the Arctic, lying in the ooze of any one of those seas where so many British ships had gone to their last resting places. That she should have survived the hazards of war was fine; that she should be up for sale just at the time when he and Calthorp had decided to pool their assets and break into the ship-owning business seemed nothing less than an omen.

" This," Barling had said, " has got to be our ship."

Calthorp had raised no objection. " If the price is right and the ship is sound, okay. We've got to start somewhere. You want to stand on that bridge again, don't you, George? It's calling you."

" It brings back memories," Barling admitted.

"Well, so long as you don't let nostalgia cloud your judgement, I don't mind. You're the one with the practical know-how and I rely on you to make the right decision."

Calthorp knew about shipping business, but not from the seaman's viewpoint; his experience had all been gained ashore, in offices where he he had become familiar with the procurement of cargoes, with marine insurance, freight charges, bills of lading and a hundred other matters connected with seaborne trade. He was a rather short, rather plump man, full of laughter, and Barling had known him since boyhood. They had been born in the same street in Harwich and had gone to school together. They had been friends ever since.

Yet it was a friendship of opposites, for Barling had always been lean, with a kind of Spartan look about him, smiling little, inclined to introspection. Where Calthorp was hail-fellow-well-met, generally at ease with strangers, Barling was reserved, giving an impression of brusqueness which those who did not know him well construed as a lack of sociability or even downright rudeness. The years, far from diminishing this reserve, seemed if anything to make it more pronounced, and the loss of his wife in a motor accident in the summer of 1966 cast a shadow on his life that time had failed to drive away.

His marriage to Mary Calthorp had strengthened his friendship with Bruce; they were now linked by an even stronger tie. But Mary's death had strained the link, for Bruce had been driving the car in which she had been killed, while Bruce himself had escaped almost unscathed. And there was more to it even than that: Barling's daughter Ann had been another passenger in the car and she had sustained injuries that had made her a cripple for life.

Barling, away on the other side of the world when the accident occurred, could not avoid a feeling of bitterness towards his partner and brother-in-law. Deep inside him there was a conviction that Calthorp was to blame; and this conviction on one side and a certain unavoidable sense of guilt on the other led to a degree of estrangement between the two men that did not augur well for the future of the partnership.

Moreover, unpalatable as it might be, there could be no blinking the fact that the venture had not been an unqualified success. The *Hopeful Enterprise* had spent too much time in dock undergoing repairs and not enough time at sea earning money. Cargoes had often been difficult to come by, and a tramp steamer insufficiently employed was an expensive piece of property.

Barling watched the wheat going into the hold, building up into little hills which men with wooden shovels levelled out. There were shifting-boards fitted fore and aft in the holds to prevent the cargo sliding over to port or starboard. It was funny stuff, grain; half-way between solid and liquid. Without the shifting-boards a roll of the ship in a heavy sea might send it pouring over to one side, causing a dangerous list.

A fine dust rose from the wheat and drifted away. It settled on the decks, on the winches, on the derricks. It moved farther afield and penetrated into the accommodation, where it laid a thin deposit on tables and chairs and bunks. Barling drew a finger along the teak rail of the bridge, pushing up a small ridge of dust. He coughed, feeling the irritation of it in his throat.

He noticed out of the corner of his eye another person standing beside him. He turned his head and saw that it was Mr. Loder, the mate, and, as always, he was irritated by the silent, almost furtive way in which the man moved, as though he found positive enjoyment in creeping up on people unobserved.

"They'll be finishing that today," Loder remarked.

Barling grunted. It had been a superfluous observation. He knew perfectly well that the loading would be completed that day, and Loder knew that he knew.

Adam Loder was about forty-five years old and as bow-legged as a jockey. He had heavy shoulders and a bullet head permanently thrust forward in a questing, inquisitive kind of way. His skin was blotchy and his mouth had a sardonic twist. The crew disliked him and it was probable that this dislike was returned in full measure and with a liberal addition of contempt, since he made no secret of the fact that he regarded seamen in general as little better than so much dirt, poor tools at best, but tools that were, unfortunately, necessary to the working of a ship.

Barling himself had no great liking for the mate and would have got rid of him long since had it not been so difficult to get an adequate replacement. Good men were not over keen to join vessels such as the *Hopeful Enterprise*; they could see no future in it. And indeed there was no future in it; for though only Barling of those on board was aware of the fact, the ship was about to set out on her last voyage under the Barling and Calthorp house flag, and possibly her last voyage of all.

Yes, it had come to that. Bruce Calthorp had decided to pull out and he had made it only too plain to Barling at their last meeting that he would not change his mind.

"We've got to face facts, George. The business isn't paying. The whole idea's been a failure and it's not worth going on."

"Give it a bit longer, Bruce. Things will pick up."

Calthorp had shaken his head. "You've been saying that for years, but you're just deluding yourself. Why not face it, George? That ship is just a big white elephant. She needs a refit, new engines, the devil and all; but she just isn't worth spending money on, even if we could raise it. No; it's one more trip and then sell out; cut our losses."

"And how much do you think the ship will make if we sell now?"

"Not much, and that's a fact. Scrap price. But if we go on we'll only lose more money. There comes a time when you have to call a halt and that time's come."

Barling knew what it was: Calthorp had lost interest in the business. They were not doing as badly as all that, but Calthorp meant to get out, come what might. Barling had heard a whisper, though Calthorp himself had not mentioned it, that his brother-in-law had had the offer of something good in the way of a seat on the board of another company. He had heard no details but he wondered just how much Calthorp was planning to invest, how much capital in fact he had apart from the half-share he would take from the wreck of the partnership; for that would not amount to a great deal. A thought came into his head, a suspicion which five years ago he would have rejected out of hand: had Calthorp been altogether honest? Had he, with his fingers on the financial side of the business, contrived to extract more than his fair share of the profits and salt away a nice little nest-egg for his own use? Barling knew that it was possible; he had trusted his partner implicitly, scarcely bothering to glance at the accounts. But had he been a little too trusting? Well, it was too late to think about that now.

"Of course," Calthorp had said, "if you want to carry on you've only got to buy me out."

It was a cynical suggestion, for he must have known that Barling was in no position to do anything of the kind.

" That's out of the question."

" Then there's only one thing for it. Sell up."

For Barling the outlook was bleak. When all debts had been settled he doubted whether there would be much left over to share between himself and Calthorp. He had no savings, no investments; and at his age it might not be easy to obtain acceptable employment. The big shipping companies had their own men and he was an outsider. He would, as it were, be starting again from scratch. And he had Ann to consider.

Ann Barling was eighteen and would never walk again. She was in a private nursing home and spent her days in a wheelchair. The nursing home was in Berkshire in pleasant country surroundings; it had every advantage except cheapness; it was very expensive indeed. Barling knew that with the break-up of the Company it would almost certainly become impossible for him to keep Ann at the nursing home where she was reasonably happy. Other arrangements would have to be made and those other arrangements would without doubt be far less satisfactory. Suppose he even found it impossible to get a job. What then was to happen to Ann?

Thinking it over now, he saw that he ought to have sued Calthorp for damages; but the idea of doing so had not even occurred to him at the time. Did one sue one's partner and brother-in-law? And there had been no suggestion then that Calthorp might be thinking of pulling out. Now it was too late.

" Madden says the engines are in poor shape," Loder remarked.

" They'll do," Barling said.

Jonah Madden was the chief engineer. For a man who earned his living in ships he had an unfortunate Christian name. He was of a gloomy disposition, perpetually moaning. He moaned to Loder about the engines, knowing that Loder would take delight in relaying these complaints to Captain Barling. Madden knew that the engines needed so many jobs done on them, needed so many parts replaced, that it would have been difficult to know where to start. He knew also that nothing would be done. He was expected to work miracles, expected to keep machinery going when the only place for it was not in a ship at all but in a scrap-metal yard. One day the miracle would fail, and that day might not be long in arriving.

"Madden is an old woman," Barling said, and regretted it at once. Loder would, of course, tell Madden and the chief engineer would be resentful.

Loder gave a sly grin; he had caught Barling in an indiscretion. "Oh, he is that; but he's right all the same. Those engines have just about had it."

"They'll do," Barling said again with a touch of bitterness. Loder did not know how little more they had to do. They would push the *Hopeful Enterprise* one more time across the Atlantic and that would be the lot. After that they could fall to bits for all he cared.

Loder shrugged. "Well, if you think so. It's not my pigeon."

"No, it's not your pigeon."

It was a dismissal, an order to the mate to mind his own business, which was above decks, not in the engine-room. There was plenty for Loder to do without bothering his head with matters that did not concern him. Though, of course, the engines were some concern of his, as they were the concern of everyone on board, since a failure in the machinery could have repercussions affecting the entire ship's company.

But Barling had more pressing matters on his mind: his future, Ann's future. The machinery would not fail; it had only to keep going for another couple of weeks, and Madden would see to that. At the end of that time he would be finished with the engines for good, perhaps finished with the sea which had been his life for nearly forty years.

Loder was still there. He was regarding his captain with a slightly quizzical expression, as though trying to read his thoughts. Barling, suddenly conscious of Loder's unwavering gaze, wondered for a moment whether the mate had somehow discovered that this was to be the last voyage of the *Hopeful Enterprise* for her present owners. Yet how could he have found out anything about that? It was a secret known only to the two partners. Unless Bruce had let something slip out. Unless the rumour had got around. Was it perhaps common talk amongst the officers and crew? Talk of which he alone was ignorant.

He looked into Loder's eyes. They were of a slaty colour, a shade too close together in Barling's opinion, with little flecks of white in the corners. Searching them for any hint that Loder knew, Barling thought he detected a trace of mockery, perhaps even of malice.

His voice, when he spoke, had a sharp edge to it. " Have you nothing to do?"

" I could maybe find something." Loder's mouth had that sardonic twist to it which always angered Barling.

" Then do so."

Loder gave a half-salute that was in itself a kind of mockery, turned and walked away. Barling watched him descend to the foredeck and speak to the bosun, a craggily built, middle-aged man named Rankin. Rankin was tall and thin, with a straggling black moustache and long arms and legs that gave the impression of being only loosely hinged to his body. He and Loder had their heads close together for about a minute like two men exchanging confidences; then Loder slapped the bosun on the shoulder and Rankin gave a neighing sort of laugh that carried to Barling's ears on the bridge. After that Rankin left the mate and walked off towards the forecastle, legs and arms swinging with no apparent co-ordination.

Barling wondered what Loder had said to the bosun to make him laugh, and again he wondered whether that rumour had gone round the ship. Or even more than a rumour. Could it be that they all knew that he was being forced to sell out at the end of the voyage? Could that have been what Loder and Rankin had found so amusing?

But why the devil should he imagine anything of the kind? Any one of a thousand things could have made Rankin laugh; it didn't have to be that.

With a muttered curse he left the bridge and went to his cabin.

TWO

FRACAS

Charlie Wilson went ashore in the evening with Sandy Moir, Aussie Lawson and Les Trubshaw. Wilson was twenty-two and the youngest of the party. He looked it too; he had a pink-cheeked, chubby face which needed shaving scarcely more than once a week and wide china-blue eyes that gave him an air of childish innocence. Secretly he was rather ashamed of his boyish appearance; he would have preferred to look mature and tough, like Lawson, the lean, rangy Australian with his long jaw and skin like old leather, or Moir, the hard-bitten Scot, whose face looked as though it had been hacked out of granite. They were real men.

He would not have wished to look like Trubshaw; that would have been going altogether too far. Trubshaw was grotesque; he stood hardly more than five feet tall, yet he had shoulders as broad as a heavyweight boxer's; his chest was like a gorilla's and you could see the muscles moving under his clothes. He was fifty years old and his face had suffered ill treatment in so many fights that what had started out as nothing to rave about even on its best days had gradually deteriorated into something calculated to give children nightmares. He had an evil temper to go with it, and those who knew him took care not to rouse it, unless they happened to be drunk or just downright reckless.

Not that Charlie Wilson was at all soft either, despite his boyish looks. He was six feet tall and well muscled, and if it came to the push he knew how to take care of himself. But he did not go looking for trouble, not like Trubshaw, or even, on occasion, Moir or Lawson. If trouble caught up with him he could handle it, but he would as soon keep out of it. Trouble meant getting hit, sometimes very hard, either with a fist or a blunt instrument or even maybe a broken bottle, and being hit with any one of those objects meant being hurt. Wilson did not enjoy being hurt; he left that to the masochists.

He had not really intended going ashore with Moir and Lawson and Trubshaw; they were not exactly pals of his, just messmates; but it so happened that they were going down the gang-plank together and Moir said: " You on your ownsome, laddie?"

Wilson admitted that he was and Lawson said: " Come and have a beer with us, chum. You could get into trouble with no one to look after you."

There was not much chance of refusing because Trubshaw had taken a grip on his arm that felt like a steel clamp and was urging him along so that he had to fall into step with the others.

" You stick with us," Trubshaw said in a voice like an old crow. " Then you can't go wrong. A young sprog like you needs to be kept on the straight an' narrer. Ain't that so, mates?"

" Too true," Lawson said, and he gave a slow wink. " If his mother was with us now she'd be begging us to keep an eye on her darling boy. There's a great big wicked city just waiting to get its claws into infants like him and it's up to us older blokes to stand between him and temptation."

"Knock it off," Wilson said. It was the kind of ribbing that touched him on the raw. "I don't need anyone to look after me. I wasn't born yesterday."

Moir shook his head in mock sadness. "Will ye listen to that. Mon, it gi'es ye no encouragement to hold out the hand o' friendship."

"The hand of friendship is mangling my arm," Wilson said. "Lay off it, Trub. What you think you're doing—arresting me?"

Trubshaw released Wilson's arm, grinning like a more than ordinarily repulsive gargoyle. "So you'll join us?"

Wilson resigned himself to a drinking bout. "Okay. I'll join you."

"That's the boy."

It started in a sleazy bar not far from the docks, the first they came to. The place was full of men with the brand of ships and the sea, mingling with longshoremen in leather caps and lumber jackets; hard men with big thirsts. Wilson knew that this was only the beginning, that they would drink a few pints and move on; the night stretched ahead of them and tomorrow the ship was due to sail.

By the time they got to the third bar they had taken the keen edge off their thirsts; they were no longer drinking to satisfy a need but to comply with a ritual.

Charlie Wilson had never acquired a real taste for this kind of thing; he got no pleasure from this systematic progress to intoxication; to him it seemed a pointless throwing away of hard-earned money. But he went along with the others because he could see no way of avoiding it. He tried to limit his own intake, but even that was difficult; Trubshaw kept an eye on him and seemed to resent any falling behind.

" Drink up, boy. You can take it."

When they reached the fifth bar Wilson was feeling sick and Trubshaw had a dangerous glint in his small, piggy eyes. He was spoiling for a fight. The others knew it, they recognised the look, but they were too drunk to care what sort of nastiness Trubshaw might stir up. They were not altogether averse to something of the kind themselves.

Wilson was the exception. He wanted no trouble; all he wanted just then was some nice quiet place to lie down and sleep.

He became conscious of another frothing glass of beer on the table in front of him. He tried to push it away. " No, thanks. Had enough."

Trubshaw's face seemed to swim across his line of vision. " Nobody's 'ad enough. Drink it, boy. Do you good."

Wilson took a pull at the beer. It tasted foul. He set the glass down, spilling beer on the table, and the room appeared to revolve, a cascade of glittering lights sailing past. He waited for the revolutions to stop, then got rather unsteadily to his feet.

" Gotta use the drain."

He set a course for the men's, made it to the door without mishap and went inside. It smelt of urine and disinfectant, the kind of smell you got in that kind of place in all the bars the world over; the only difference with this one was that it smelt worse than most, a little above the average in pungency.

He was sick and after that he felt slightly better. He wiped his mouth on his handkerchief and went back to the others with a filthy taste on his tongue.

Lawson was trying to roll a cigarette and the tobacco was falling into his beer. When it was finished it was about as thick as an under-nourished tapeworm. It flared up when he lit it and burnt his nose. He dropped it on the floor and ground it angrily under his heel.

Moir examined Wilson with bloodshot eyes. " Ye dinna look so guid, laddie."

" I don't feel so good," Wilson said.

" What ye need's a dram."

" I don't need a dram."

" Are ye bloody contradicting me, laddie?" Moir thrust his granite face towards Wilson, jaw jutting belligerently. Like Trubshaw he had taken enough to make his temper uncertain

" I'm telling you I don't need a dram," Wilson said. For two pins he would have pushed Moir's face in. He was not feeling very friendly. He had not wanted to go drinking with the three of them in the first place. They had dragged him in and now he felt like death. To hell with them.

Moir seemed inclined to carry the argument further but finally decided not to. He gave a grunt and withdrew his face to a more reasonable distance.

There were four big, fair-haired men standing by the bar, drinking beer and talking loudly in some language that was certainly not English and did not sound like French either. They were laughing a great deal and the sound of their laughter drew Lawson's attention. He turned his head and stared at the fair-haired men. Then he said very distinctly: " Poles."

The men heard him. They stopped laughing and turned away from the bar to face the table where Lawson and his companions were sitting. One of them walked over to the table and said: " No, not Poles. Swedish. From Swedish ship. You English, huh?" He sounded friendly.

" I'm Australian," Lawson said. " These here yobs are English."

" That's a bloody lie," Moir said. " Ah'm Scottish."

Lawson acknowledged the correction with a flip of the hand. " Sorry, chum. I forgot."

" What you drink?" the Swede asked.

Trubshaw looked at him in surprise. " Are you payin' mate?"

" I pay," the Swede said. " We join you, no? All seamen, all from ships. Stick together."

" Suits me," Trubshaw said. The offer of a drink seemed to have put him in a better humour. " Plenty room at this table."

The Swede called his countrymen over, and they all sat down and eight more glasses of beer appeared on the table. Only two of the Swedes could speak English; the other two communicated by signs and grins. The one who had bought the beer introduced himself as Olaf Brondsted; the others were Johannes Vigfusson, Carl Jonsson and Eric Andersen. Lawson did the introduction for himself and his party. They all shook hands.

" We arrive today," Brondsted said. " From Hamburg. You been here long?"

" Long enough," Lawson said. " We sail tomorrow. *Hopeful Enterprise*. Wheat."

" *Hopeful Enterprise*? You from that ship?"

" That's right. You know her?"

" We see her," Brondsted said. He relayed this information to the two who did not speak English. One of them said something in his own language and they all laughed.

" What's so bleedin' funny?" Trubshaw demanded. " What'd 'e say?"

" He say *Hopeful Enterprise* very old ship."

" What if she is? I seen older."

" Is nothing. Is just that our ship very new."

"You think that's funny?" Trubshaw was speaking slowly and deliberately, and Wilson could sense the tension beginning to build up. Moir was looking angry too. The Swedes had stopped laughing. "You think you're flamin' superior or sumfin, jus' 'cause you got a newer flamin' ship?"

"I do not say that." Brondsted was keeping his voice under control but his face had hardened. "I think you take offence too easy, my friend."

"Friend!" Trubshaw said. "What makes you think I'm your friend? Jus' 'cause you buy the drinks don't make me no friend o' yours, an' don't you forget it."

Brondsted was still keeping his voice low, but there was an edge to it. "Are you wishing to pick a quarrel?"

It was Lawson who broke the tension. "Ah, forget it, chum. Drink up, can't yer? What're we arguing about? Sure, the *Hopeful Enterprise* is old. She's a bloody old worn-out crate. What in hell's it matter? Forget it, Trub. Drink your beer. Next round's on me."

Trubshaw muttered something under his breath, but he drained his glass and everybody relaxed. Wilson breathed more easily with the crisis passed, but he knew that it might well be no more than a temporary respite with Trubshaw in his present mood. Nevertheless, for two more rounds things seemed to go smoothly enough, even though Trubshaw said little, sitting with his elbows on the table, drinking his beer and staring at the Swedes with unconcealed resentment.

Strangely, it was Wilson himself who was the cause of the unpleasantness flaring up again. He had not been drinking and there were now three full glasses of beer in front of him. Jonsson, the other English-speaking Swede, who had just bought a round, leaned across the table and said: "Why you not drink?"

" I've had enough," Wilson said. " I don't want any more."

" But I buy you beer."

" Give it to somebody else. Drink it yourself."

" No," Jonsson said. " I buy you beer, you drink."

Wilson had the feeling that he had had this kind of argument before—with Trubshaw and Moir. Why in hell couldn't people leave him alone? Why in hell should he drink if he didn't want to?

" Nobody tells me what to do."

Jonsson was the biggest of the Swedes and looked the oldest. He had a scar like a starfish on his left cheek. " So you insult me, no?"

" I don't insult you."

" You don't drink beer I buy, you insult me."

" Okay then," Wilson said wearily. " So I insult you. Now what are you going to make of it?"

Jonsson brought his fist down on the table, making the glasses jump. " Nobody insult me like that. Nobody."

" Ah, fer Chrissake," Trubshaw broke in, " whyn't you leave the kid alone? If 'e don't wanter drink, why should 'e flamin' well drink? It's a free flamin' country, innit?"

Which was pretty rich coming from Trubshaw, Wilson thought.

" He insult me," Jonsson said again. He had a slow, stolid way of speaking and he looked the kind of man who would get an idea into his head and keep it there against all argument. " He don't drink the beer I buy."

" So what you goin' to do abaht it?"

" What I do about it?" Jonsson thought that one over and seemed stumped for a suitable answer.

" If you're so flamin' bothered abaht it," Trubshaw said,

" why don't yer do what the kid said? Drink the pissin' stuff yerself." He stretched out a hand and slid the glass of beer across the table to Jonsson.

Jonsson looked at the glass and then at Trubshaw. He had ice-blue eyes and high cheek-bones, and like all of them he had drunk enough to make his temper uncertain. He pushed the glass slowly back towards Wilson.

" I say he drink it."

It could have gone on a long time like that, but Trubshaw did not let it. " No," he said. " You flamin' drink it." And he picked up the glass in one massive hand and flung the beer in Jonsson's face.

The barman was there so fast he must have jumped over the counter. He was a chunky, bald-headed man wearing a striped shirt and a bow tie.

" Cut it out," he said. " You wanna fight, you go out-side. You try anything in here and I'll have the cops on you so quick you'll wonder what hit you."

Mention of the police had a sobering effect. Jonsson took out a handkerchief and wiped the beer from his face. He looked at Trubshaw and he said in a hard, slow voice: " We go outside. We find a place. Okay?"

" Suits me," Trubshaw said.

Brondsted stood up. " Maybe we all go outside."

" Are you looking for a fight too?" Lawson asked.

" We have all been insulted."

Lawson grinned. " Well, if that's the way you feel, chum. You go first. We'll follow."

Charlie Wilson sighed. He could see himself being dragged into a fight now, a fight in which he had no desire to be involved. Damn Trubshaw; damn Jonsson; damn the lot of them. If he could have seen a way of getting out of it he would have done so. Theoretically he could have stayed where he was, could have refused to go with the others; they could not have forced him to go. But that was not really a practical proposition for the simple reason that he shared a mess with Trubshaw and Lawson and Moir. He could imagine only too well what life on board the *Hopeful Enterprise* would be like for him if he chickened out of the fight, if he refused to help his shipmates in this senseless quarrel with the Swedish seamen.

The Swedes all got up, drained their glasses and went out of the bar in a compact group.

Trubshaw finished his beer and stood up. " Come on then. Wotcher waitin' for? "

" Crazy bastard," Wilson said. But he stood up too.

The Swedes were waiting for them. When they got outside the Swedes turned and walked away up the street. They followed.

They were in the old part of the city and there were buildings with fire-escapes climbing up them like a kind of iron creeper. There were some signs by the kerb reading, " Ne stationnez pas ", and others which read " No parking "; and Wilson's eye was caught by an advertisement for a brand of whisky that was new to him. The night was fine and cars went sweeping past, but there were few pedestrians. It was easy to keep the Swedish party in sight.

After about two hundred yards the Swedes stopped, glanced back to see that the others were still following, then turned off to the right. They seemed to know where they were going, so perhaps they had been in Montreal before. When the *Hopeful Enterprise* party reached the turning they saw that the Swedes were some thirty yards ahead in a narrow street lighted here and there by lamps on tall iron standards. A moment later the men had disappeared as though suddenly swallowed up by the night.

"Now where've they gone?" Trubshaw said. "They tryin' t'give us the slip?"

But he had no cause for worry on that score. The Swedes were waiting for them in a kind of courtyard or small square on the other side of a brick archway between two tall buildings. The square was poorly lighted and was enclosed by four- and five-storey houses, probably used as apartments or offices. It was a good place for a fight; it was secluded and apparently deserted; they were not likely to be interrupted.

The Swedes had halted and were waiting for them. Wilson felt more impressed than ever by the sheer stupidity of the whole affair. What were they preparing to fight about? An argument over whether or not a man should drink a beer he did not want. Could anything have been more foolish? They were grown men, not children. Yet with drink in them they became like children; except that they were far more dangerous.

"Come on then," Trubshaw said. "Let's be gettin' stuck into the bastards."

He rushed at Jonsson, whom he had obviously picked out as his particular assignment, and aimed a vicious blow at the Swede's stomach. Lawson and Moir closed in also, taking on Brondsted and Vigfusson respectively. That left Andersen for Wilson to deal with.

Wilson did not rush forward with the other three; he stayed where he was, about ten yards from the Swedes, and looked at Andersen. Andersen was a handsome man; he grinned at Wilson and said something unintelligible which might have been an invitation to come in and mix it. He seemed to be quite good-humoured about the whole business, unlike Jonsson and Trubshaw, who were both needled and in deadly earnest. Wilson had a feeling that, in different

circumstances, he could have got along very well with
Andersen, and he wondered what Andersen would do if he
offered to shake hands. Why shouldn't the two of them stand
aside and watch the others fighting it out? He had little
desire to hit Andersen and even less to be hit by him.

Out of the corner of his eye he saw that Jonsson and
Trubshaw were on the ground and that Trubshaw seemed
to be trying to grind his opponent's face into the rough
paving of the square. The other two pairs were slugging
away at one another with the obvious intention of inflicting
as much bodily damage as possible and with little regard
for the arts or rules of boxing. It looked exactly what it was:
a nasty, vicious, unscientific affray.

Wilson looked at Andersen as much as to say: " What are
you and I doing in this set-up?"

Andersen said something else that Wilson did not understand, then walked towards Wilson, grinning and holding
out his right hand. So he had the same idea; he also wanted
to shake hands and let the others get on with the argument
if they wished. With a feeling of relief Wilson held out his
own hand and took a couple of paces towards Andersen.

Their hands met and clasped. Andersen had a powerful
grip and, too late, Wilson discovered that he had fallen into
a trap. He felt himself being jerked suddenly forward, and
then Andersen's clenched left fist struck him on the side of
the jaw with crushing force. Something seemed to explode
inside his head and for a moment he was blinded by stars.
He staggered, but Andersen was still gripping his right hand
and would not let him go. Instead, Andersen kicked him
on the left shin.

The pain was agonising. He wrenched his hand away
from Andersen and heard the other man laugh. Wilson
burned with anger so hot that it almost drove out the pain.

It was a dirty way to fight, a dirty trick to play. And there was no reason for it. What had he ever done to Andersen?

He could hear the sounds of the fight that was taking place—cries, curses, thuds, gasps for breath; but he no longer had time to stand aside and observe; he was involved now, whether he wished to be or not. Now he had to fight.

He caught a glimpse of Andersen's foot swinging at him again, and he swayed aside and caught Andersen's ankle in both his hands. He gave a jerk and Andersen went over backwards and landed heavily. Wilson ran in and stabbed at Andersen's throat with the toe of his right shoe. Two could play at that game.

But his balance and judgement of distance were not as good as they might have been, not with the amount of alcohol he was carrying in his system. He missed the throat and hit the shoulder. Andersen was hurt, but not nearly as badly hurt as he would have been if the kick had gone to the intended target. He was up in a moment, but his right arm must have been numbed by the shoulder kick, for it hung nervelessly and he retreated towards the far side of the square away from the entrance, trying to keep his distance from Wilson until the life came back into his arm.

Wilson followed closely, striking at Andersen with his right fist. But again his judgement of distance was at fault and he failed to make contact. Andersen, still retreating, was finally brought to a halt by a brick wall at his back. Wilson closed with him, got his left arm round Andersen's neck and began driving in short, jabbing punches with his right. Andersen tried again to kick him, but this time Wilson was prepared for it and dodged aside. In so doing, however, he lost his balance and fell over, dragging Andersen down on top of him. For a while they struggled inconclusively on the ground, both breathing hard, each trying to gain some advantage but without much success.

It could have gone on much longer if there had not been an interruption. The interruption brought the conflict to an abrupt conclusion. Wilson heard a car stop in the archway, blocking the entrance to the yard. A number of policemen got out and there were some more behind them, probably from another car.

Andersen jumped up and made a run for it. One of the policemen stuck out a foot, tripped him up and hit him with a night-stick. Andersen made no further attempt to get away.

The one who was apparently in charge of the police said in a tired kind of voice: " Okay, fellers, that's enough. Break it up. You've had your fun."

Wilson got slowly to his feet. Trubshaw and the others were between him and the police, and where he was standing there was a good deal of shadow. He pressed himself back against the wall, still panting from his exertions and feeling bad. He could see no way of escape; the entrance to the square was well and truly blocked and if there was an alleyway or anything of that kind on this side it was not visible to him. Behind him and on each side the houses loomed like cliffs.

" Come on now. Let's have you, fellers," the policeman said. " Nice an' quiet now. You make no trouble, we make no trouble. Okay?"

Trubshaw gave a jeering laugh. " You want us to make it easy for yer? To 'ell wi' that. Come on, boys; it's time ter go."

He made a rush at the police, head down like a charging bull. The others hesitated momentarily, then followed. In an instant police and seamen were locked together in a struggling mass just inside the entrance.

No one was paying any attention to Wilson and he had no intention of making himself conspicuous by joining in the struggle. Let Trubshaw and his pals and the Swedes, now united against the common enemy, work that one out for themselves. If only he could find a way out on this side of the square he might still manage to avoid arrest.

He was still thinking about it when he felt a hand tugging at his arm, and a woman's voice, low and urgent, said: " This way, sailor. Follow me. Hurry now."

THREE

A SWEET BOY

WILSON DID not waste time in futile questions; he allowed himself to be led to an unlighted doorway only a few yards to the right, stepped over the threshold into utter darkness and heard the door close behind him.

There was a faintly sour odour, as of damp timber. Wilson stood perfectly still like a man who fears that if he takes one step he may fall over the edge of an unseen precipice. He wondered who had called the police, but it was not important. He heard the woman's voice again.

"There should be a light but it's burnt out. Just keep close to me. There's some stairs."

The stairs were bare wood. There were banisters on the left and a wall on the right, as his hand discovered. He kept close behind the woman and they came to a landing. He heard a door creak open and the snap of a switch. Light flooded out from the doorway.

"Well, don't stand there," the woman said. "Come in."

He went in and she closed the door. He saw that she was about thirty, maybe older, blonde, overweight, wearing a black skirt and a white nylon blouse. She had a wide mouth and a lot of eye shadow and imitation pearl earrings.

"You'd better tell me your name," she said. "It'll make things simpler."

" Wilson."

It was an untidy room, cheaply furnished, a television set occupying one corner. An inner door, standing ajar, gave access to a bedroom; he could see part of the bed and a dressing-table. There was a kind of alcove containing an electric cooker, a sink and cupboards.

" I can't call you Wilson. You've got another name?"

" Charlie."

" Well, hello Charlie. I'm Bobbie."

It was, he thought, the kind of name she would have. But he said nothing. He was still feeling sick and his head ached. His jaw hurt where Andersen had hit it; his shin too.

" Like to tell me what it was all about?"

" Just a fight."

" I heard it. And then the police came."

" Then the police came."

" They don't like people to have fun."

" It wasn't fun."

" No? You don't like fighting?"

" There's no point to it."

She gave him a searching look. " I don't think you're feeling so good. Why don't you sit down?"

" Thanks."

The chair creaked under his weight. Bobbie stood with hands on hips, facing him. The skirt was tight, revealing the curve of her thighs.

" You're English, aren't you?"

" That's right."

" And a sailor?"

" It's what you called me."

" It was a guess. You look like a sailor."

" And you? You're not French-Canadian?"

She gave a laugh. " With this accent? Hell, I don't even

speak French. I'm from Toronto. Surname, if you really want to know, Clayton."

" Bobbie Clayton. Nice name."

" Who are you kidding?" She was still gazing at him, as if weighing him up. " My, you're lucky being a sailor."

" What's so lucky about that?"

" No ties. When you're good and ready just pull up stakes and go."

" Nobody's bound to stay where he is."

" Sure, that's the theory. Doesn't always work though."

" You left Toronto."

" And landed up here in this dump. You want some coffee?"

It was what he needed; his head throbbed and his jaw felt as though a good job of sabotage had been done on it. The Swede could certainly hit hard even if he did fight dirty.

" Thanks. I could do with a cup of coffee."

" It's what I thought. You had some drinks, I guess."

" Some."

She moved to the alcove and got busy with the coffee-making. Wilson wondered whether any of the others had got away. He doubted it. Perhaps, like the woman said, he was lucky. He didn't feel lucky.

" I wonder," she said, " why men always get so goddam violent when they're drunk."

" I don't get violent."

" You were fighting out there, weren't you?"

" I was dragged into it."

" Oh."

He closed his eyes and lay back in the chair. He was almost asleep when he felt her hand on his arm. She had a steaming cup of coffee in her other hand, strong and black.

" No milk?"

" This will do you more good. And, boy, you need something."

She left the cup in his hand and crossed to the other side of the room. She sat down on a sofa that looked as though it had taken a beating in its time and tucked her legs under her, kicking off the shoes as she did so.

" You want to stay the night here?"

Wilson sipped his coffee. " How much will that cost me?"

She gave a laugh and he could see her breasts shaking under the nylon blouse. " You're a careful one. What was it worth to be rescued from the coppers?"

Wilson made no answer. He had nearly one hundred and fifty Canadian dollars in his wallet. He had drawn the money against his pay with the intention of buying a suit and other clothing in Montreal, but he had never got round to doing so. He had no intention of letting Bobbie Clayton know how well heeled he was.

" So that was why you brought me in from the cold."

" Would you rather I'd left you to the cops?"

" Don't think I'm not grateful," Wilson said. " He drank some more of the coffee and thought about money. He put the cup down on the floor and took the wallet out of his pocket. He opened it and extracted fifty dollars. Bobbie was watching him. He hoped she could not see how much money there was left, but he was afraid she might have caught a glimpse of it. He put the wallet back in his pocket, got up from the chair, walked across to the sofa and laid the dollars on Bobbie's thigh.

She looked up at him, smiling. " You're a sweet boy."

" Don't call me that," Wilson said, and he sounded angry.

She picked up the dollars, folded the bills and stuffed

them down the back of the sofa. "You don't like it?" She seemed surprised.

"I'm not a boy."

"No," she said. She caught his hands in hers and pulled him towards her. "I can see that."

She released his hands, put her arms around his neck and drew his head down to hers.

He could smell the scent of her and his brain whirled with a new intoxication. Then she had brought their mouths together and her lips were moving on his. His heart was thudding in his chest like a hammer. She turned her head aside and he kissed her throat, her blonde hair brushing across his eyes.

"Take it easy," she said. She put her hands on his chest and pushed him away. "No need to hurry. Finish your coffee. We've got all night, you know."

Reluctantly he moved away from her, went back to his chair and drank the coffee.

"You want another cup?"

The fumes of alcohol were still floating round in his head and his stomach was queasy. Perhaps more coffee was what he needed.

"Yes," he said, "I'll have another cup."

This time she fetched a cup for herself too. She sat on the sofa drinking it and gazing at him with a trace of amusement in her eyes.

"What's so funny?" Wilson demanded.

"I was just thinking."

"Thinking what?"

"It doesn't matter. How old are you, Charlie?"

His head jerked. "What's it to you?"

"Nothing. I just wondered. You look—"

"What do I look?"

" You look—well—young."

He had been half expecting her to say that he looked like a boy. He might have hit her if she had. Perhaps she had read the warning in his face.

" I'm twenty-four."

" That's young."

" It's old enough."

" Yes, it's old enough." She sounded regretful. " I'll never be twenty-four again."

" You're not so old."

She gave an ironical sort of laugh. " Well, thanks for the compliment." She sipped her coffee. " When do you sail?"

" Tomorrow."

" So soon? Looks like we shan't be seeing each other again after tonight."

" I could be back. You'll still be here?"

She cast a glance round the room and answered wryly: " Sure, I'll still be here. I'm not going places."

She finished her coffee and put the empty cup on a nearby table. She leaned back against the end of the sofa and pushed the hair away from her face with a sweep of the hand. Wilson watched her and felt an overpowering desire to hold her again in his arms, and to be held by her. He set his own cup down so clumsily that it turned over in the saucer, spilling coffee.

" You don't have to throw it around even if you don't want it," Bobbie said.

He did not answer. He got up from the chair and walked over to the sofa. He went down on his knees in front of it and put his arms round her waist. He pulled her towards him and buried his face in the soft hollow between her breasts.

He felt her hand touching the back of his head, fingers

gently stroking his hair. There was a constriction in his chest as though an iron band were tightening about it. For some reason that he could not understand he wanted to cry like a child, and a few dry sobs shook him, tearing free of that constricted chest.

The fingers continued to caress his head. " There, now," she said, and her voice had an unusual gentleness in it, as though she were indeed speaking to a child. " There, there."

He awoke in the night and his mouth was parched. He had been dreaming and the dream was still in his mind, the vision of it still not wiped out by the reality of waking. It had been a nightmare of fire at sea, a recurrent fear that he had. The fire had driven him to dive from the ship, but it had followed him, oil burning on the surface of the water, searing his throat. Then he had awakened, sweating and dry-mouthed, not knowing where he was or how he had got there.

Then gradually the nightmare faded and he remembered. He remembered where he was, whose bed he was lying in, all that had happened the previous evening. He lay on his back, eyes closed, thinking of the woman, of Bobbie, of how good she had been to him. What did it matter that she had done it for money? He believed that there was more to it than that; he wanted to believe so, to believe that she had some real feeling for him beyond the purely mercenary aspect.

Wilson had never known his father or mother, only a variety of foster-parents. Perhaps he was still searching for the kind of affection of which he had been robbed in childhood, prepared to find it anywhere, even in the most unlikely of places. It made him vulnerable.

He rolled over on to his side and stretched out his left

hand, searching for the woman. The bed was still warm where she had been lying, but she was not there. Wilson opened his eyes and became aware of a light in the room, a dim, shaded light coming from below the level of the mattress. He twisted across the bed and peered over the edge.

It was the lamp from the bedside table and it was standing on the floor with the flex trailing. There was a black nylon slip draped over the shade in order to dim the light, but there was enough shining through to reveal to Wilson what was going on.

Bobbie was crouched down by the chair where his clothes were piled and she had something in her hand. When he saw that it was his wallet and that already she had opened it and was in the act of pulling out the remaining hundred dollars he did not want to believe it. It smashed everything, every illusion he had had. That was what hurt; he would have given her the money rather than have this happen. He wanted to hold on to the belief that she really had some genuine affection for him, however small. She had made him think that, but he could see now that it had been nothing but a sham; all she had ever wanted was his money.

"Damn you!" he said, and it was more a groan than a cry. It came from the bitterness of his disillusionment.

She looked at him, still crouching there, naked; still with the money in her hand and the blonde, disordered hair hanging down over her shoulders.

"You should have stayed asleep, Charlie. It would have been better."

There was a trace of annoyance in her voice, as though she were accusing him of some lack of consideration, blaming him for any embarrassment the situation might cause. She appeared to have no feeling of shame at being discovered in the act of stealing, nor did she show any sign of fear.

" Yes," he said bitterly. " I should have, shouldn't I?"

Her coolness served only to increase his anger, and he felt sick in the stomach.

She stood up. " I hope you're not going to do anything silly. After all, it's only money."

" If you'd asked me I'd have given it to you. You didn't have to steal it."

She shook her head. " Oh, no, Charlie. You wouldn't have done that. Not you."

" I would. You had only to ask."

Light and shadow fell on her naked skin. Wilson stared at the voluptuous curves of her body and felt a sudden overwhelming impulse to hurt her, to punish her for what she had done to him. He clenched his fists, grinding the nails into the palms of his hands, striving to control himself.

She stared back at him mockingly. " Well, I'm asking you now. Can I have the money?"

" It's too late," he shouted. He would not have her laughing at him, taunting him. " Damn you! Can't you see it's too late?"

He flung back the blankets and swung his legs over the edge of the bed, his face working. At last she seemed to have a suspicion of the demon she had aroused in him and to feel afraid. She stepped back a pace.

" No, Charlie. Don't be a fool."

He leaned forward and slapped her on the left cheek. The blow made a sound like a whip cracking, but she did not cry out.

" Okay," she said viciously. " Take your goddam money if it means so much to you." And she flung the wallet at him.

Some of the dollars came out and fluttered to the floor. The corner of the wallet hit Wilson in the eye, then fell to the floor also. The sting of the impact served to inflame his anger even more. He reached out and gripped the woman's neck with both hands, pressing his thumbs into her throat. She made a choking sound and tried to struggle free, beating at his face and chest with her clenched fists.

Wilson scarcely felt the blows. It seemed as though a gong were reverberating in his head. Bobbie's face was distorted, her mouth open, eyes bulging. His thumbs still pressed relentlessly into her throat.

He became conscious only slowly of the fact that she had ceased to struggle. He felt the weight of her body dragging at his arms. He lowered her carefully to the floor and stood up.

Only then did the full realisation of what he had done get through to him. He had killed her. Oh, God, he had killed this woman! The utter irrevocableness of the act struck him like a blow. He felt trapped; from this horror there could be no escape.

A glimmer of hope came to him. Perhaps she was not dead; perhaps she was merely unconscious and could be revived. If that were so, if only he could bring her to her senses, she could have all the money. More; he would send her more; he would pay anything, anything, just to have this terrible load lifted from his mind.

He dropped to his knees beside her, raised her left wrist and tried to find the pulse. Nothing. He put his ear against her side, listening for the beat of her heart. He could not hear it. He lifted his head and looked at her face. It had darkened and there were bruises on the neck where his hands had gripped. Her eyes were open and they seemed to be staring at him.

"No," he muttered. "No, you're not dead. You can't be."

He began to shake her. "Wake up, Bobbie! Wake up!" He was sobbing like a child that has broken its favourite toy in a fit of anger and knows no way of mending it.

The woman's head rolled from side to side. He seized the blonde hair and pulled the head towards him. "Bobbie, speak to me. I didn't mean to hurt you. I'm sorry. But just speak to me. Say something, Bobbie, say something."

It was useless. He allowed the head to drop back to the floor and stood up. He was shivering uncontrollably and he felt cold and weak. What was he to do? He tried to think, but his brain refused to work coherently; it kept panicking; he had an impulse to run out of the apartment, naked as he was, and just keep running.

But he resisted the impulse. He began to dress and gradually became a little more composed. He looked at his watch; it was nearly two o'clock. For a few moments he stood perfectly still, listening. He could hear no sound in the building; if there were other people in other apartments they were obviously asleep. The killing had made very little noise; Bobbie had not even screamed when he smacked her face and the brief struggle had been utterly soundless. There was no reason why anyone should have had the slightest suspicion of what was taking place.

He bent down and gathered up the scattered money. He slipped the bills into the wallet and stowed the wallet in his pocket. He looked down at the nude body and was disgusted by the sight. There was something almost obscene about it. He pulled a blanket off the bed and draped it over the woman.

He made a careful inspection of the room to make sure that he had left nothing, then he switched off the light, groped his way to the window and drew back the curtains. A little weak light filtered in. He crossed to the door, carefully avoiding the body, went into the other room and closed the door behind him. Here too he drew the curtains back before opening the outer door. There was a key on the inside. He transferred it to the outside, stepped out on to the landing, closed the door very softly, locked it and dropped the key into his pocket.

The landing was in utter darkness, but he remembered the lay-out. He began to move cautiously towards the stairs, feeling ahead with his foot. He found the top step, then got his hand on the banisters and started to descend. A board creaked loudly and he froze. He heard a lavatory flushing somewhere, but no light showed. He descended two more steps and heard the door open below him.

Wilson froze again, his right hand gripping the banister rail. Someone came in with a gust of cold night air and he could see the vague outline of a bulky figure in the doorway. There was the snap of a switch but no light came on. Wilson heard a curse and it was a man's voice. Then the door slammed shut with a violence that seemed to shake the building. The man was obviously annoyed about the failed light and was taking it out on the door.

With the door shut Wilson could no longer see the newcomer, but he could hear him muttering to himself. If he came up the stairs he would be certain to bump into Wilson. So would it be advisable to retreat and slip back into Bobbie's apartment? Yet if he moved the man might hear him and might be suspicious. Wilson did nothing. He waited.

Suddenly there was a spark in the darkness below and then the flicker of a small flame. The man had ignited a cigarette lighter and was holding it in his hand like a miniature torch. The wavering flame revealed a large, pale face and wide mouth. The man was swaying slightly and Wilson guessed that he was half drunk. He had only to glance up and he must see Wilson, and then there was no telling what might happen; drunks were unpredictable. He might start shouting, kicking up enough noise to rouse everyone in the building.

For perhaps half a minute the man remained where he was, swaying gently, the lighter wavering in his left hand. Then he moved towards the staircase. He caught the bottom post of the banisters in his right hand and again came to a halt. Wilson remained perfectly still and waited for the inevitable discovery when the man began to climb the stairs.

But that did not happen. The man pushed himself off the banisters and went blundering down the passage beyond the staircase. Wilson heard him trip over something that sounded like a bucket and there was another flow of curses. Then a door banged and the place was again in darkness.

Wilson descended the last few steps and groped his way to the door. He had no idea what he would do if he found it locked; he would then be trapped in the building and would have to wait until someone opened it up in the morning. He felt sick at the thought.

His fingers, searching in the darkness, found the doorknob. He turned it and pulled. The door swung open. The drunk had forgotten to re-lock it.

Outside the square was deserted. Wilson slipped away like a thief, through the archway, into the street, meeting no one. He forced himself not to run, though the impulse was there and was almost irresistible. He still felt cold and sick and afraid, but he walked at a steady, unhurried pace in the direction of the harbour and the ship which now seemed to call to him as a refuge.

A police patrol car came up behind him. It slowed and his heart began hammering. He tried to think what he would say if they were to question him, to ask where he had been. He ought to have prepared some story but it had not occurred to him and now he could think of nothing; the fearful truth filled his mind to the exclusion of all else. Suppose he were to blurt it out, unable to control his tongue. The mere possibility made him tremble.

The patrol car crawled up beside him, keeping pace. He did not turn his head. The nearside window of the car was wound down.

"Just a minute, feller."

Wilson stopped. The patrol car had stopped too. He walked towards it, his legs feeling weak and the sickness in his stomach.

"Where you goin', feller?"

There were two of them in the car. The one who was doing the talking had a heavy jowl with the dark shadow of a quick-growing beard, the kind of face that needed three shaves a day.

"I'm going back to my ship." Wilson's mouth was dry; the words seemed to come with difficulty.

"Sailor, huh?"

"Yes."

"You're out late."

"Yes."

"What's your name?"

"Charles Wilson." It had come out automatically. No time to think of a false name.

"What ship?"

Wilson tried to think of some other ship and nothing came of it. "Hopeful Enterprise."

The policeman appeared to think it over, staring at

Wilson with hard, suspicious eyes. Wilson could see no reason why he should be suspected of wrong-doing, but coppers were like that; it was their job to suspect everyone —especially at half-past two in the morning.

" Hopeful Enterprise, huh?" He turned to his companion sitting behind the wheel. " Say, Joe, you heard that name before?"

The other man grinned. " I'll say." He leaned across and spoke to Wilson. " Sailor, we got some shipmates of yours cooling off in the lock-up."

" Oh," Wilson said. He had clean forgotten Trubshaw and the others, the original cause of all his troubles. He remembered them now with no feeling of sympathy.

" They were misbehaving themselves," the first policeman said. They both seemed to find it amusing. Perhaps they had not been directly involved and could afford to take a detached view. " Lucky you weren't with them."

" Yes," Wilson said. " Lucky."

The policeman gave him another long, searching look and seemed to find nothing he could really fasten on to. Then he said: " We're going your way. You want a ride?"

" Thanks. I'd rather walk."

" Guilty conscience?"

Wilson tried to laugh, but it was a poor effort. " No. I've got a headache. Need some fresh air."

" Okay. Please yourself. Take her away, Joe."

The patrol car moved off and Wilson stood on the sidewalk shaking, the sweat cold and clammy under his armpits and on his forehead. He took a deep, shuddering breath and walked on.

He dropped the key to Bobbie's apartment into the gap between the ship and the side of the wharf. It made a faint plopping sound as it hit the water.

FOUR

NO PROMISES

THE WHEAT lay in the holds. It had been finally levelled off by the men with the wooden shovels and the imprints that their feet had made could be seen on the golden surface of the grain.

A winch was clattering. The heavy steel beam of number three hatch was being lowered into position, men guiding it at each end. It dropped lower, settled into place; the lifting wire slackened and was unhooked. The first hatch-board was lifted from the pile by the bulwarks, carried to the hatch and dropped home, its upper side snugly level with the coaming. One after another the massive boards were fitted in until the wheat could no longer be seen. Then the heavy tarpaulin was unfolded, stretched over the boards and battened down.

Charlie Wilson, knocking wedges in along the coaming, felt ill. He had crawled into his bunk in the crew's quarters some time after three in the morning, but he had not slept. He had lain there in the darkness listening to the snores of the other men and seeing in his mind's eye the dead woman stretched out on the floor of her room. He wondered when the body would be discovered. It could lie there for days before the other inhabitants of the building began to wonder why they were not seeing Bobbie around any more. By then the *Hopeful Enterprise* would be hundreds of miles away and there would be nothing to connect the crime with him.

Nothing? What about fingerprints? His fingerprints must be all over the apartment, and he had not even given it a thought until that moment. What a fool! What a damned fool! He ought to have wiped everything he had touched. He could have done so, but it was too late now; he could not go back. And those policemen in the patrol car: they would remember him when the murder came out, and then they would put two and two together. And they knew his name and the name of his ship. He would be arrested as soon as the *Hopeful Enterprise* reached England; there would be an extradition order and he would be sent back to Canada to stand trial.

He could scarcely touch his breakfast; it seemed to stick in his throat. And then there was the ribbing that he had to face.

" Rough night, Charlie?"

" I've got a headache."

" Too bad. A young lad like you oughter lay off the booze."

" It wasn't the booze."

" No? Maybe it was the women."

Their mindless laughter grated on his nerves; the fug in the seamen's mess sickened him; he could have cried out in his misery.

" Poor old Charlie; he can't take it. Well, he's only a kid when all's said and done."

He felt an urge to shout at them: " Leave me alone! Leave me alone, can't you?" But he said nothing. It would do no good. He had to endure.

Rankin the bosun was another person who was not in the

best of humours that morning. With the *Hopeful Enterprise* making ready to leave, there was a fistful of work to be done, and now it seemed that three men were missing, three able seamen whose muscles were going to be badly needed to help get everything sorted out. He stormed into the mess-room, arms and legs swinging loosely.

" Anybody seen Trubshaw, Lawson and Moir?"

Someone volunteered the information that they had not slept on board.

" Damn them," Rankin said, chewing savagely at the ends of his moustache. " Damn their perishin' guts. They should've been aboard by six this morning. Where in hell they got to? In some stinkin' whore-shop, I'll wager."

Wilson could have told the bosun that was not true, but he held his tongue.

" Anyone know where they went?" Rankin demanded, swivelling his gaze round the mess and letting it rest momentarily on each man in turn. " Any of you lot go ashore with the bastards?"

A man with a broken nose and not much in the way of teeth pointed a finger at Wilson. " Charlie went with 'em. I seen 'im. They was all together, them three an' 'im."

Rankin looked at Wilson. " That true?"

" Well, yes, bose," Wilson admitted. " But I didn't stay with them. We split up."

" You know where they went after that?"

" Well, I did hear something."

" What did you hear? Come on, lad. Out with it."

" I heard they were in the nick. For causing a disturbance."

" So why in flamin' hell didn't you say so at once?"

Wilson said nothing.

" In the nick," Rankin muttered. " It's what we might've

expected." He shot another glance at Wilson. "How'd you come to hear about it if you'd left them?"

"A couple of policemen told me. At least, they said some of my shipmates were locked up. They didn't say who they were, but it must be Trub and Aussie and Sandy if they're adrift."

"I don't get it," Rankin said. "Why would a couple of cops go out of their way to tell you about it?"

"It's a long story." It was a story Wilson had no intention of relating to the bosun or anyone else. "It doesn't matter."

Rankin looked like a man who had much to bear and was doing his best not to lose his self-control. "Why in hell didn't you report it straightaway? You know we're due to sail."

"I didn't think of it."

"Didn't think of it! Well, if that don't beat everything. Wait'll I tell the mate about this. He'll blow his top."

Rankin turned and went out of the messroom like a perambulating windmill to spread the bad news in Mr. Loder's direction.

Captain Barling heard a knock on his cabin door and called: "Come in."

Adam Loder walked in, cap under arm, heavy shoulders and bullet head thrust forward.

Barling gave a slight lift of the eyebrows. "Well?"

"There's three men adrift, so the bosun tells me. It seems they're in gaol."

Barling was less stirred by this news than Loder had expected. It rather took the wind out of Loder's sails.

"I know. I've just heard from the Police Department. Seems the three men were drunk and fighting with some Swedes. They resisted arrest too."

" Which is what might have been expected. So what do we do? Sail without them? Leave them to stew?"

Barling filled and lighted a pipe. " I'd rather like to, but I think not. We need those men; we don't want to sail short-handed."

" You mean we wait here until they're let out?"

" It won't be long. I gather that they'll be charged this morning. They'll be fined of course. I want you to go along, pay the fines and bring those men straight back here."

Loder was not at all pleased with his commission. " You wouldn't like me to hold their hands?"

Barling ignored the sarcasm. " The fines will, of course, be stopped out of their pay."

Loder hesitated. Barling said with a touch of asperity: " Well, what are you waiting for?"

A faint tinge of colour crept into Loder's blotchy cheeks and a glitter of resentment appeared in his slate-grey eyes. " Able seamen!" he said disgustedly. " They haven't the ability to wipe their own bloody noses. They need bloody wet nursing."

He turned abruptly and went out of the cabin.

A few minutes later Barling had another visitor: Jonah Madden, the chief engineer. Barling knew without having to ask what Madden had come about. There was only one subject that seemed to hold any interest for the chief and that was the subject of the decrepit engines of the *Hopeful Enterprise*.

Madden looked a bit decrepit himself. He was pushing sixty, hollow-chested, with a face like a discouraged bloodhound and a chronic wheeze of the kind that heavy cigarette-smokers often got; which was rather unfair, seeing that he never smoked. Perhaps the wheeziness was the result of many years of exposure to the tainted atmosphere of ships' engine-rooms; perhaps the oil had settled on his lungs.

Madden said gloomily: " I won't guarantee it."

Barling looked at Madden in mild inquiry. It was a cryptic remark, typical of the man. " Won't guarantee what, Chief?"

" That they'll carry us across the Atlantic."

" Meaning, I take it, your precious engines?"

They were in fact Barling's engines; at least, fifty per cent of them, the other half being Calthorp's; but Madden, as long as he was chief engineer, had a kind of courtesy title to them and could not have been more concerned about them had they indeed been his.

" Yes," Madden said, wheezing more heavily than usual. " My precious engines."

" They'll make it," Barling assured him. " You worry too much." He wondered, not without a touch of embarrassment, whether Loder had relayed that unguarded remark of his about Madden's being an old woman.

Madden picked at his nose, which had a spongy appearance about the end. " There's reason to worry, if you ask me. Suppose we hit dirty weather—which is more than likely at this time of year, you must admit—it'll put an extra strain on them."

Barling looked Madden fairly and squarely in the eyes. " Are you telling me, Chief, that those engines are incapable of driving this ship back to England?"

Madden's eyes shied away like frightened fawns. He had been driven into a corner and he knew it. He temporised. " I'm not saying that exactly. Maybe they will." He seemed to pick up courage and his gaze came back and held Barling's for a moment. " But I'm telling you this: if they don't have a proper overhaul in our next port I won't be responsible for what happens on another voyage, and that's the truth."

Barling thought about that. It occurred to him that Madden would scarcely have made such a statement if he had had any idea that the ship would not be going on another voyage. So perhaps, after all, the rumour had not got around. Unless Madden was fishing. Barling searched Madden's face and could find no hint there of anything but the usual nagging worry.

" Chief," he said, " I give you my word that this is the last voyage I'll take in this ship with the engines as they are. Now, does that satisfy you?"

Madden shuffled his feet. " I'd be happier if they'd already been seen to, but maybe they'll get us through just this one more crossing." He sounded slightly mollified by Barling's statement.

" You'll see that they do."

" I'm making no promises. I'm not a magician."

" You're a very good engineer and that's enough for me. I'm relying on you. And I'll tell you this—there's no one in the world I'd have more confidence in than Jonah Madden."

Sometimes you had to use flattery. He saw Madden square his narrow shoulders.

" Well, I'll do my best."

" That's all I'm asking."

Madden went away and Barling was left to his own worries. Loder and Madden, they hadn't got the burden that lay on his shoulders.

Trubshaw, Lawson and Moir arrived back on board midway through the morning looking not at all chastened by their night in captivity. They had some bruises and

Lawson's upper lip was cut, but otherwise they seemed little the worse for their experience; in fact, they seemed to regard it as a huge joke.

" What 'appened to you, Charlie boy?" Trubshaw asked when he saw Wilson. " Ow'd you manage to give them coppers the slip?"

" I hid."

" Well you crafty young so-and-so. I didn't see no place in that square where a flea could 'ide."

" I kept in the shadow. They were so busy with you lot they didn't notice me."

" Well, ain't you the lucky one." Trubshaw shook his head, marvelling at Wilson's good fortune. " You must 'ave someone up there lookin' arter you."

" Yes," Wilson said. " I expect I have."

He remembered that Bobbie also had called him lucky. What kind of a joke was that?

The *Hopeful Enterprise* moved out into the stream and headed down-river with a Canadian pilot guiding her, a small, pinched man in a lumber-jacket and a leather cap. The cargo of wheat weighed the ship down and water lapped the load line, the keel biting deep. Madden's precious engines were working, turning the massive propeller shaft in its tunnel under the decks, but Madden was not happy; he had a premonition of trouble ahead; he felt it in his bones. The other engineers laughed at him behind his back, referring to him disrespectfully as Old Worryguts. The imperfections of the ship's machinery did not bother them. But they were younger men and the responsibility was not theirs. To Jonah Madden responsibility was a cross that he had to bear.

So, with the screw pushing them and the current helping,

they went floating down the St. Lawrence, slipping past the hazards that the pilot knew like his own face, past the small towns and the little wooden churches, past river steamers and motor launches and rowing-boats and all the wide variety of scum and flotsam that is borne on the broad back of a mighty river. And Wilson could think of nothing but the nude body of a blonde woman lying under a blanket in a room in Montreal. Or perhaps no longer lying there; perhaps discovered, removed to a mortuary, the hunt for the killer already on. Perhaps the message had been flashed down to Quebec to intercept the *Hopeful Enterprise* and arrest Able Seaman Charles Wilson on a charge of murder. Wilson felt sick at the thought; he went about his work with his mind on other things and earned the bosun's rebukes for his clumsiness.

"What in hell are you dreaming about?" Rankin demanded. "You're in a bloody trance. It's about time you got that bird out of your mind."

Wilson glanced at Rankin in sudden alarm. "What bird? What are you talking about?"

"I'm talking about the one that's taking your mind off your work, that's the one."

Wilson gripped the bosun's arm. "What do you know about her?"

Rankin brushed Wilson's hand away. "So that is the trouble with you. I thought as much. Well, take my advice, son, and forget about her. There's none of 'em worth bothering your head over, none of 'em. I'm telling you."

Wilson saw with relief that Rankin knew nothing. How could he possibly have known? That remark about the bird had just been a random shot that had happened to strike home.

"Yes, bose," Wilson said. "I expect you're right." He

was becoming altogether too sensitive and jumpy; if he went on like this he would give himself away; already he had become conscious of some questioning looks being turned on him in the mess. He had better watch it; the last thing he wanted was to arouse curiosity. Yet it was difficult to behave naturally when there was that monstrous cloud hanging over him.

He looked forward with gloomy foreboding to the time when the ship would arrive at Quebec, for that was where he feared the police would come on board and take him. And there was no way of escaping them; in the *Hopeful Enterprise* he was as much a prisoner as he would have been in gaol. He was helpless, unable to do anything but wait for them to come and get him.

It was morning when they reached Quebec. The carpenter, a heavy-limbed, black-bearded man named Orwell, stood by the steam windlass on the forecastle and let the anchor go with a great rattling of chain through the hawse-pipe. The ship swung with the current and finished with her stern pointing downstream. Wilson, under the bosun's direction, lowered a Jacob's-ladder over the side and saw the pilot-boat heading out from the shore. There was nothing in that to cause him any disquiet; it was normal procedure to change pilots at Quebec. But a moment later he saw the police launch and his heart began to hammer.

The launch was coming straight for the *Hopeful Enterprise* and there was no doubt at all in Wilson's mind that it was coming for him. He could see the police uniforms and he had an impulse to rush to the other side of the ship, jump overboard and swim for the opposite shore. But what good would that do? They would catch him before he could get half-way. There was nothing he could do, nothing.

" Oh, God!" he muttered. " Oh, God help me!"

He gripped the top of the bulwark and pressed his forehead to the cold iron, trembling.

A hand fell on his shoulder. He looked up and saw the bosun staring at him in no very friendly fashion.

" What's up with you now? Taking forty bloody winks?"

" I feel sick."

" Sick! So am I. Sick of useless tools like you."

The pilot-boat had reached the ship. The new pilot began to climb the Jacob's-ladder. Wilson saw that the police launch was less than fifty yards away. Suppose he were to run away and hide. But where? In the bilges? In one of the lifeboats? In the chain locker? All equally futile. They would find him wherever he was. It was inevitable.

Rankin snarled an order and Wilson moved as if in a trance. He could hear the stammer of the engine of the police launch and it seemed to be beating a tattoo in his brain. It came closer, louder, then, unbelievably, began to decrease. The launch slipped past the stern of the *Hopeful Enterprise* and moved away.

Wilson felt weak with relief; there was sweat on his forehead and his hands were shaking. They had not been coming for him after all. So perhaps the body had not yet been discovered. He clutched gladly at this small reprieve and the receding sound of the launch was like sweet music in his ears.

Not so sweet was the bosun's impatient voice snarling at him. " You're dreaming again. Get moving."

Wilson got moving.

FIVE

RUMOUR

THE *Hopeful Enterprise* hauled up her anchor and left
Quebec astern. The St. Lawrence widened like a funnel with
the water pouring through it in the wrong direction, and
they steamed along the northern curve of the shore between
Anticosti Island and the mainland, through the narrow Belle
Isle Strait and out into the broad Atlantic.

And Madden's engines had not given a single moment's
cause for alarm—except to Madden himself, who looked
upon even the smoothness of their working as an evil omen,
a sinister design on the part of that ill-favoured machinery
to lull him into a false sense of security before springing the
trap.

" It's not going to last," he confided to Mr. Loder. " It's
all going a sight too easily. But we're not home yet, not by
a long chalk. There'll be a day of reckoning."

The mate did not bother to disagree. Madden's fussing
provided him with a good deal of malicious amusement,
and he was not above throwing in a word or two to fan the
chief engineer's resentment at Barling's failure to pay sufficient attention to the needs of the engine-room.

" Perhaps," Loder said, " there's a day of reckoning
coming for George Barling too. And not so very far away
at that."

Madden's gloomy eyes stared at Loder and his eyebrows went up like animated question-marks. " And what might you be meaning by that?"

Loder dropped his voice to a conspiratorial level. " I fancy there's a crash coming for the Barling and Calthorp line."

Madden looked even gloomier. "You've heard something?"

" No, I haven't heard anything. I'm just using my own powers of observation and deduction. It's sticking out a mile. What do B. and C. add up to when all's said and done? One rusty old ship with worn-out engines."

" They may have other assets."

" Do you believe that?" Loder gripped Madden's lapel and pulled him closer; so close that he could see in detail all the unsightly blotches that littered the surface of Loder's face like so many bits of rubbish littering a public park after a Bank Holiday. " Do you think if they had there'd be all this penny-pinching over ship's stores? Dammit, they don't buy enough paint to keep an auxiliary ketch in decent trim."

" So you really think they're going under?"

" I look at the signs, and if you want my opinion they all point that way." He drew Madden even closer, so that their noses almost touched. " It seems to me, Chief, that you and I are likely to be looking for new berths before we're very much older."

Madden put a hand on Loder's chest and pushed him away. The mate was a little too close to be pleasant; his breath was offensive and what he was saying had a depressing effect on the chief engineer. Madden had no desire to go looking for a new appointment; in his heart of hearts he was not at all certain that he could get one, not at his age.

He had hoped to serve out his time with Barling and Calthorp, whatever the shortcomings of that company might be regarding engine overhauls. But if Loder's deductions were correct it looked as though Barling himself might soon be on the beach, and that was a dismal outlook indeed.

"You could be wrong," he said, but without conviction.

"I could be, but I don't think I am. Everything points that way, everything. If you've been counting on new boilers, Chief, or anything in that line, my advice to you is to forget it."

"Barling promised—" Madden began.

"Yes?" Loder cocked his head on one side. "What did he promise?"

"He said this was the last trip he'd be taking in this ship with the engines like they are. He—" Madden stopped again, aghast at the sudden realisation of the double meaning those words could have had.

Loder was quick to seize on this revelation. "He said that, did he?"

"Something of the kind."

"Well now, that's interesting; that's very interesting indeed. It bears out just what I've been saying."

"I don't see—"

Loder gave his twisted smile. "Oh, but I think you do, Chief. I think you see very well. Don't you?"

Madden turned away. He did see, and he did not wish to. It was too bleak a prospect.

"Last voyage for the *Hopeful Enterprise*," Loder said softly. "Make the most of it."

At about the same time as the *Hopeful Enterprise* was leaving Montreal a much newer ship was setting out from Philadelphia with a cargo of electrical and other machinery destined for Reykjavik in Iceland. The s.s. *India Star* was a vessel of 8,700 tons owned by a Greek millionaire, registered in Monrovia, flying the Liberian flag, manned by an Asiatic crew and commanded by a Dutch captain named van Donck.

The fact that the *India Star*, by reason of her higher cruising speed and the course on which she was steaming, would, if all went according to plan for both ships, pass within a hundred miles or less of the *Hopeful Enterprise* somewhere between the thirtieth and fortieth parallels of longitude, was something of which neither Captain Barling nor Captain van Donck was aware. Not that the knowledge, even had they possessed it, would have been likely to excite either of them to any noticeable extent, since it was in the natural order of things that ships should pass other ships even in mid-ocean at no great distance. Yet to Barling at least the fact was to be of the utmost interest, and the *India Star*, of which he had scarcely even heard, was destined to float into his life and occupy a place of supreme importance in his plans.

But all that was yet several days ahead, and as he stood on the bridge of his ship gazing at the grey wastes of the North Atlantic his thoughts were only of the uncertain future, of his daughter Ann and what was to happen to her when Barling and Calthorp went into liquidation and he was thrown up on the beach with nothing but a few hundred pounds to call his own. His thoughts were sombre indeed, the thoughts of a man who sees that all his labours, all his schemes, all his expectations have ended in one thing—failure. And he was at the age when the realisation of failure is perhaps hardest to bear. A younger man could have started again with fresh hope; an older man might have accepted the situation with resignation; he could do neither.

As the *Hopeful Enterprise* headed eastward the weather was good, the winds moderate and the sea unusually calm for the time of year. The much maligned engines continued to give no trouble, despite Madden's forebodings, and the ship steamed on at a steady speed of ten knots, while the patent log, streaming from the taffrail, reeled off the long sea miles of this last ocean voyage of the thirty-year-old vessel so that they might be recorded faithfully to the end.

Watches came and went, the chronometer was adjusted to the changing longitude, and all the set routine of a ship at sea was carried out from day to day. Now and then memories of an earlier voyage drifted into Barling's mind, and looking down from the bridge he remembered the Bofors gun in the bows and the paravanes lying under the bulwarks; he remembered the degaussing cables and the Lewis guns and the black-out curtains. There had been company in those days, a small city of ships keeping together for mutual protection, the destroyers and corvettes out on the perimeter and maybe an armed merchant cruiser in the centre; sometimes a Sunderland or a Catalina circling round if you were near enough to base; zigzagging, the continual flutter of signal flags and pennants, the winking of Aldis lamps, the rumble of depth-charges and the sudden explosion in the night bringing the heart into the mouth.

Dangerous times; the threat of death constantly there; and yet he had loved it. He had been young then; he had had youth and had taken it all in his stride. Now he was older; the ship was older; the guns had gone and the convoys had dispersed. Above all, youth had gone. It would never be the same again.

It was two days after they had lost sight of land when

Jonah Madden came to Barling's cabin. Madden had come ostensibly to report that all was well so far in his department. Barling had not asked for a report and there was no reason why Madden should have made one at that particular time; but the real purpose of the chief engineer's visit was a rather different one: he wanted information. Ever since his talk with Loder the question had been nagging him: were Barling and Calthorp going down the drain? He could not sleep for worrying about it; it plagued his mind; it even made him sick in the stomach. He could not remain in suspense any longer; he had to know for certain, one way or the other. That was why he had come to see Barling.

Yet, now that he was there, he still found difficulty in getting to the point. It was not the kind of question you asked a man straight out. Madden lingered, remarked on the strangely clement weather, other inconsequential matters, wearing out Barling's patience.

" What's on your mind, Chief?"

" On my mind?" Madden was startled, blissfully unaware that he had been revealing any uneasiness. " What makes you think there's anything on my mind?"

" There's always something on your mind," Barling said. " It's usually engines. But you've just told me there's no trouble there, so it must be something else."

Madden rubbed his nose, cleared his throat and stared hard at a framed photograph of the *Hopeful Enterprise* screwed to the bulkhead, a photograph he had seen many times before and could have little interest in now. " It's a bit delicate."

" What is? Your health?"

" No," Madden said, taking the question with perfect seriousness. " I'm in good shape physically."

Barling would have considered that highly questionable,

but he did not say so. He said: " I'm glad to hear it. So if it's not your health that's delicate, what is?"

Madden cleared his throat again and turned his melancholy eyes on Barling. " The question I want to ask you."

" Oh, yes. What question?"

Madden coughed. " There's a rumour."

Barling's chin jerked up. So it was out. He did not need to be told what rumour, but he asked just the same.

" Well," Madden said, " there's talk that you may be—er—retiring."

He was putting it as tactfully as he could.

Barling's eyes probed his, and Barling had the kind of eyes that seemed to be capable of digging very deeply; hard, steely, disconcerting when you were forced to look into them, as Madden was at that moment.

" No more than that?" Barling asked.

Madden wriggled his shoulders, distinctly uncomfortable. " There's a bit more. The way I heard it—and I'm not saying I believe it—but the way I heard it is that the Company is—er—going out of business."

" Why don't you say what you really mean?" Barling's voice had become as hard and steely as his eyes. " Why don't you say you think Barling and Calthorp are on the rocks? That they're going bust."

" I don't think that."

" Don't you? Are you quite sure you don't?"

Madden did not know where to look. He tried to avoid Barling's eyes. " Of course I'm sure."

" Well, that's nice to know." Barling's tone was faintly sarcastic. " As the sole representative of the Company present, I thank you for your vote of confidence."

Madden flushed. " You don't have to take it like that."

Barling felt that perhaps he had been a little rough with

the chief engineer. It did not require any very deep insight to see why Madden was worried; he was no more eager to go looking for a new job than Barling himself was. He was seeking reassurance, almost begging for it. And that, unfortunately, was just what Barling could not give.

" I suppose you've been talking to Adam Loder?"

" I did have a word or two with him."

It was as Barling would have guessed: Loder had sniffed out something or had deduced it from observation. And then he had passed on his conclusions to poor old Madden, knowing that the merest hint of anything of that kind would be enough to worry the chief engineer sick. It was like Loder. He would have to get rid of that man, engage a new chief mate.

But that was a stupid idea; after this trip he would not be needing a mate or any other officers; he would not be engaging anyone. And Loder would be laughing up his sleeve, not caring a damn about the loss of his own position if it meant the downfall of his superior. That would please him; it was the kind of mean-minded character he was.

" So he told you B. and C. were finished?"

" No, no; he didn't say that, not exactly." Madden looked alarmed. " You mustn't think—"

" I'll decide what I may or may not think," Barling said curtly. " And let me tell you this: I don't confide the Company's business to you, to Mr. Loder or to anyone else. Is that clear?"

Madden looked hurt; he was like a whipped dog, a dog unjustly whipped. Barling felt a twinge of conscience; Madden had reason to be concerned; after all, his future was at stake too. But it would not have helped to tell him the truth; this way at least he could hope, even if the hope must be short-lived.

" Is there anything else you wished to speak to me about, Chief?"

" No," Madden said. " Nothing else."

He walked to the door and left the cabin, shoulders hunched. One thing was certain: his mind was very far from having been put at ease.

Charlie Wilson's mind was not at ease either. He had watched with a feeling of relief the land fading astern; but even the knowledge that he was away from Canada, more than a thousand miles from the scene of his crime, could not banish the fear that held him in its grip. The day of reckoning had not been eliminated; it had simply been postponed.

He wondered whether there had been any signal over the radio concerning the affair, a warning perhaps that Able Seaman Wilson was wanted in Montreal on a murder charge and was to be watched. They would not tell him, of course; it might be kept a secret between the radio officer and Captain Barling, not even shared with the other officers.

Wilson made a point of intercepting the radio officer whenever the opportunity occurred, trying to read in his face any hint that he knew something. Mr. Scotton was a young, slightly-built man with very fair hair and a silky beard that looked sadly under-nourished. He had a habit of stroking the beard with his left hand, perhaps in the belief that a course of massage might encourage growth, but the results were disappointing. Mr. Loder had been heard to remark that Sparks's beard was beyond hope and that the best thing to do would be to shave it off and give it a decent burial at sea, because it would never amount to anything. But Scotton was a persevering young man and refused to give up.

He was also extremely polite, and whenever Wilson managed to cross his path and mutter some form of greeting he would smile and nod in a friendly sort of way, and Wilson would spend the next few hours trying to decide whether there had been some hidden meaning in that smile. Had Sparks perhaps been smiling because he knew?

Wilson, plagued by uncertainty, was almost driven to asking him outright whether there had been any signal concerning a murder in Montreal. And in fact on one occasion he did go so far as to stop Scotton with the intention of making an attempt to get some information from him in a roundabout way. But when it came to the point he found it impossible to do anything but make some futile remark on an altogether different subject, leaving Scotton gazing at him in a rather puzzled manner, as though suspecting that Wilson was not quite right in the head.

In the seamen's mess his moodiness had become a subject for comment. Things finally came to a head when Trubshaw, leaning across the long, narrow table that was bolted to the deck and had swivel chairs on each side of it, said: " What's eatin' you, Charlie boy?"

" Nothing's eating me," Wilson said. " What makes you think there is."

Trubshaw drank some tea to wash down the food he had been taking on board, belched loudly and said: " Because you bin lookin' like a bloody dyin' duck ever since we left Montreal, that's why."

" I can look how I please, can't I?" Wilson felt a surge of resentment. What had it got to do with Trubshaw how he looked? " It's none of your business, is it?"

" None o' my business? Well, that depends on the way you look at it. An' the way I look at it's like this 'ere. When there's a messmate o' mine goin' about all day wiv a face as sour as a pint o' milk left out in the sun it affects me. It makes me feel as 'ow life ain't as good as it oughter be, an' I don't like that. So I'm askin' you again—what's eatin' you?"

"And I'm telling you again," Wilson said, his voice rising. "Mind your own damned business. I don't poke my nose into your affairs, so keep your big nose out of mine."

Trubshaw's scarred and ill-used face turned red with anger. Nobody talked to him like that, nobody; least of all this young whippersnapper who was still sucking his mother's tits when he, Trubshaw, had already been in fights from Buenos Aires to Singapore and from Hong Kong to San Francisco. Who in hell did he think he was with his baby face and his sulks?

"Why, you—" Trubshaw said; and he stood up and reached across the table with his long, gorilla-like arms and took two large handfuls of the front of Wilson's blue jersey. "Why, you cheeky young bastard. I'll learn you to talk to me like that." He pulled Wilson towards him across the table, dragging him down on to the remains of the recently concluded meal, the dirty plates and bits of bread, the cups and the sauce bottles. "'O d'you think you are? Givin' yerself airs, aincher?"

Wilson had been fed up with Trubshaw already, and this indignity suffered in front of a messroom half full of grinning seamen was the last straw. At any other time the older man's evil reputation might have been enough to deter him, but now he was in no mood to care about reputations. Moreover, it was Trubshaw he blamed for all his misery; if Trubshaw had not coerced him into going out on the booze with him and Lawson and Moir; if Trubshaw had not picked a quarrel with the Swedes, all would have been well; there would have been no fight, no police, and he would not have met Bobbie Clayton. He would not have killed her.

" Damn you!" he shouted. " Damn your rotten eyes!" He felt his groping right hand make contact with an enamel pie-dish, still containing the congealed residue of an Irish stew. Without a second thought he picked it up and smashed it into Trubshaw's face.

Trubshaw gave a yell and released his hold on Wilson's jersey. Wilson pulled himself away from the table and stepped back against the bulkhead behind him, watching Trubshaw, a little apprehensive now that the heat of the moment had passed.

There was silence in the messroom. No one was saying a word. Everyone was looking at Trubshaw and waiting to see what he would do to Wilson.

Trubshaw wiped the stew from his face and stared across the table at Wilson with his little, piggy eyes. He said nothing either; he just began to walk round the table. The others made way for him.

Wilson watched Trubshaw coming and did not move. He knew that he was no match for this broad, squat tank of a man; nobody in the ship was. Trubshaw could kill him with his bare hands if he had a mind to do so. And that, judging by the expression on his face, might well be just what he did have a mind to do.

And might it not be the best way out? It would solve everything. No more wondering whether the body had been found and whether the police were on to him; no more nightmares in which he strangled the woman again and again, and from which he woke sweating and shuddering; all that would be finished if Trubshaw killed him.

But he knew, just the same, that he did not want to die, that he would fight Trubshaw if he had to fight him with every ounce of strength in his body, every last gasp of breath in his lungs. And he knew also that, whatever he did, Trubshaw would win, because that was the way it had to be.

Trubshaw had reached the end of the table and was edging between it and the sink with the water heater above it and the plate racks and the lockers. He was not moving fast but with a solid deliberation that was somehow far more menacing than any bull-like rush would have been.

Wilson said, breaking the silence: " You asked for it."

Trubshaw did not answer.

" You started it," Wilson said. " You grabbed me." He looked at the others for confirmation. " You all saw him, didn't you?"

Nobody said anything. They were not taking sides against Trubshaw.

Trubshaw walked towards Wilson, down between the backs of the chairs and the side of the messroom. The ship rolled a little and a glimpse of sea was visible through the portholes with their screwed-down covers, a plateau of broken water heaving up into view and then sinking away again. The roll did not affect Trubshaw's stability; he had spent half his life in ships and he knew their ways.

" Keep away from me, Trub," Wilson said. " I'm warning you."

" An' I'm warning you, sonny boy," Trubshaw said; and he drove his clenched fist into Wilson's stomach.

Wilson was slammed against the bulkhead as if a battering-ram had struck him. He could not breathe; he wanted to be sick; he knew that he ought to be fighting back, ought to be hitting Trubshaw, but his arms refused to do anything about it. He could see a fragment of meat clinging to Trubshaw's hair and gravy on the side of his face and on his shoulder. And Trubshaw was grinning, a sadistic kind of grin, as if he were beginning to enjoy himself and meant to go on doing so.

He hit Wilson again, on the side of the jaw, and Wilson's legs began to fold. Trubshaw hit him a third time before he reached the deck and then started kicking him.

Wilson rolled over, pain stabbing at him. He struck upward blindly and felt his fist bury itself in the softness of Trubshaw's groin, felt it go in deep, all his desperation driving it.

It stopped Trubshaw. It stopped the kicking. Wilson managed to get himself up into a sitting posture, his back against one of the chairs, his head singing. Trubshaw was doubled up, not grinning now, but with his mouth twisted into a grimace of agony. Wilson had really hurt him.

Again there was silence in the messroom, broken only by the creaking of timber, the rattle of cutlery, and a laboured, grunting noise coming from Trubshaw. Wilson looked at Trubshaw and was scared, scared of what Trubshaw would do to him when he recovered from that punch in the groin. He thought about getting away, but Trubshaw was between him and the door. And even if he escaped from the messroom, where would he go? Once more the hard fact forced itself upon him: in a ship at sea there was nowhere to go.

Trubshaw straightened up slowly, carefully, as though testing the way before committing himself. When he had reached his full height of five feet nothing he moved towards Wilson. Wilson got up quickly and backed away. Trubshaw followed. Wilson retreated until he was brought to a halt by the end bulkhead of the messroom. Trubshaw came to a halt too and stood looking at Wilson.

" I'm goin' to make you sorry you done that," he said. " I'm goin' to smash you, kid. Oh, yes, I'm really goin' to smash you now. When I've finished with you you're goin' to need plastic surgery."

This time Wilson did not wait for Trubshaw to start things; he put his head down and rushed at the other man, arms flailing, fists beating at Trubshaw's iron face like hailstones rattling against a brick wall, and with little greater effect. Trubshaw gave a shake of the head like a horse bothered by flies, then slugged Wilson with a left and a right to the stomach. Wilson went down again, retching, and once again Trubshaw began to kick him systematically, without passion, but with a deadly accuracy, picking his targets.

" Give it a rest, Trub," Lawson said. He sounded worried. " The kid's had enough. You wanter kill him?"

Trubshaw paused in his kicking and stared at Lawson. " Keep out of this, Aussie, 'less you want a sample of it yerself."

Lawson's mouth tightened. It looked for a moment as though he might be about to take Trubshaw up on that; but he thought better of it.

" You'll kill him," he said, but he made no move to stop the killing.

" Maybe I will," Trubshaw said, and he started kicking Wilson again.

Wilson could taste the blood in his mouth and his jaw felt as though it might be cracked. His whole body seemed to be on fire, nothing but pain and more pain as the kicks exploded in his quivering flesh. Oh, God! he thought, when will it end? Oh, God, make it end!

It went on.

When he thought about it afterwards Wilson could not help wondering whether Trubshaw would have gone on until he had really kicked the life out of his victim. It was possible; for Trubshaw had a kind of brute mentality that did not look beyond the immediate moment, did not consider the possible consequences of any action. So he would probably have gone on kicking Wilson until there was no life left in the boy, not because he had any real desire to kill him but simply because he was in the mood to take his revenge by inflicting pain. Wilson had dared to provoke him and for that must take his punishment; that was Trubshaw's code.

That he did not in fact kick Wilson to death or at best permanent injury was not the result of any change of heart but simply the intervention of Orwell, the black-bearded carpenter. Orwell, passing the doorway of the messroom, looked in and saw what was happening. And he did not like what he saw. In fact he liked it so little that he went into the messroom at a quicker pace than was normal with him.

The first that Trubshaw knew of Orwell's presence was a heavy hand on his shoulder and a voice bellowing in his ear: " Give over!"

Trubshaw stopped kicking Wilson and turned to face the carpenter, breathing hard from exertion and anger. " Get your bleedin' 'and off my shoulder."

Orwell drew his hand away without haste. " Are you trying to kill the lad?"

" It's nothing to do with you, Chippie. You keep out of this."

" Nowt to do with me, is it? Well now, I don't happen to agree. I'd say it's to do with anybody when a young lad's being hammered senseless." He looked at the other men and there was contempt in his eyes. " Why were you lot letting this go on? Haven't you got any spirit in you? Why didn't you stop it?"

They shifted their feet uneasily and avoided his eyes, but said nothing.

Trubshaw sneered. " They knew they couldn't stop it. No more than you can."

" Ah, but I can," Orwell said. " And I will."

Trubshaw said, coldly menacing: " Get away from me, Chippie. Don't try to stop me or it'll be the worse for you. I'm goin' to learn that young cub some manners, and not you nor nobody else ain't stoppin' me."

" I'm stopping you, Trub," Orwell said, and he moved in between Trubshaw and Wilson. " I'm stopping you."

" Are you lookin' for a fight too?" Trubshaw sounded surprised. He thrust his chin out belligerently. " Cos if so, that's what you can 'ave."

" I'll not fight with you," Orwell said. " I'm not daft."

" Then get out of the way, an' stay out."

Orwell stood his ground. " I'm not moving. You let him be. I'm telling you."

" And I'm tellin' you, Chippie—" Trubshaw made a move to thrust Orwell aside and found a wide-bladed knife with its point no more than an inch from his stomach.

" Don't start anything, Trub," Orwell said. The knife had been in a pigskin sheath on the back of his belt and again he had moved more swiftly than was usual with him.

Trubshaw glanced down at the knife and then up at Orwell. The carpenter overtopped him by more than a foot. " You wouldn't do it."

" Want to try me?"

Trubshaw looked as though he would have liked to do so but could not quite bring himself to the mark. The muscles on each side of his jaw stood out, iron-hard, as he clenched his teeth.

" When it comes to a choice betwixt sticking a knife into

your guts and being beat up," Orwell said evenly, " it's the knife every time for me."

Trubshaw stared into Orwell's eyes, clenching and unclenching his fists. And Orwell stared coolly back at him, the knife held firmly in his right hand. It was obvious to everyone present that he was perfectly prepared to sink the blade into Trubshaw's belly if such an action should become necessary.

It must finally have become obvious to Trubshaw also. He gave a harsh laugh that sounded more than a little forced. " Okay, Chippie, 'ave it your way. You can put that knife back where you found it. I've finished with the kid. I reckon I've learnt 'im 'is lesson anyway."

He moved to a chair and sat down, took a tin of tobacco and papers from his pocket, and began to roll a cigarette.

The tension eased. Men started talking again. Orwell slipped the knife back into its sheath and helped Wilson to his feet. The incident was ended.

SIX

ERRAND OF MERCY

IT WAS nine days since the *Hopeful Enterprise* had left Montreal, and in all that time the weather had been good, the engines had given no trouble, and to all appearances there had been nothing to worry even the most nervous of men. Yet, in spite of everything, there were worried men on board: no amount of good weather could ease Barling's mind as the days passed and the moment drew inexorably nearer when the ship must be sold and the Company go into liquidation. Nor were the engines now Jonah Madden's sole, or even chief, concern; for what did it matter about engines if this was to be the last voyage? And all things pointed to the probability that it was.

The third worried man was Charlie Wilson, still gloomily anticipating inevitable arrest when the ship reached England. The effects of his beating-up bothered him less; the stiffness in his limbs, the bruises all over his body, the cuts on his face—all these were painful enough, but they were merely physical pains from which he would recover, and indeed recover quickly, since he had the resilience of youth on his side; but the other trouble was in a different class; from that there was no recovery; it simply got worse.

Barling was not too preoccupied with his own affairs to notice Wilson's injuries. Wilson's face was not a pretty sight.

Barling mentioned the fact to Loder and instructed the mate to find out what had happened.

Loder made inquiries and brought back a report. " He tripped over on the deck and hit his face on a winch."

Barling stared hard at Loder. " Do you believe that?"

" It's what I was told."

" That's not what I asked you."

Loder shrugged. " Does it matter?"

" That boy looks to me as if he'd been in a fight."

" It's possible."

" I don't like brawling in my ship."

A faint smile appeared to flicker across Loder's blotchy face. It was gone in a moment, but Barling detected it and guessed the cause: no doubt Loder was thinking that it might not be his ship for much longer.

" There's another matter I've been meaning to speak to you about," he said.

" Yes?" Loder's eyes seemed to mock him.

" I think you've been spreading rumours."

" Rumours?"

" One rumour. I think you know what it is."

" I'd like you to tell me."

Barling controlled his temper with some difficulty. " Did you or did you not tell Madden that the Company was going down the drain?"

" By Company I take it you mean Barling and Calthorp?"

" Of course."

" Well," Loder said, " I can't recall my exact words, but I wouldn't say I told him that—not as a fact."

" You said you believed it was so."

" Did he tell you that?"

" Yes."

" Then maybe I did. I'd hate to call Jonah a liar."

" What right have you to go around spreading tales of that sort?"

" Oh, come now; let's not call it spreading a tale." Loder was smiling his crooked smile, which infuriated Barling. " Let's just say I was voicing a legitimate suspicion."

" Legitimate?"

" Oh, yes, I think it could be called that, all things considered. But of course, if there's nothing to it, I'll be only too pleased to tell Madden so. Just give me that assurance and I'll be happy to pass it on. I'm sure it will relieve his mind a great deal."

Barling wanted to hit Loder; it took all his self-control to avoid doing so. But it would never have done to give vent to his anger in that way, though perhaps it was just what Loder would have liked. Loder had him in a corner and they both knew it. Without lying, he could not give any assurance that the Company was not going into liquidation, and he would not lower himself to giving the direct lie. As he had done in his interview with Madden, he resorted to a refusal to be drawn into any discussion of the affairs of Barling and Calthorp.

" My advice to you is to wait and see."

Loder nodded, still with that infuriating smile on his lips. " I'll do that. Yes, that's just what I will do."

He turned away and left Barling to his none too pleasant thoughts.

Wilson was avoiding Trubshaw as much as possible; he did not wish to be drawn into any more arguments with that hard, vicious man. One experience of that kind was enough to last for a very long time indeed. Not that Trubshaw himself showed any inclination to resume hostilities; he had had time to cool down, and probably considered that he had taught Wilson his lesson thoroughly enough. He grinned when he saw Wilson's bruised and swollen face the next morning and indulged in some heavy banter.

" Wotcher bin doin', kid? 'Avin' an argument with the wrong end of a mule?"

Wilson did not answer.

" Lost your tongue too? Well, ain't that just too bad." He gave Wilson a smack on the shoulder. " Never mind, kid; you'll get over it."

Wilson knew that; he did not need Trubshaw's assurance. But there was that other matter which Trubshaw knew nothing about; he would not get over that. Ever.

Towards Orwell Trubshaw's manner was different. He looked darkly at the carpenter but said nothing. Orwell had pulled a knife on him and had humiliated him in front of witnesses. That he would not forget. That he would never forgive.

So, for nine days, apart from these outbreaks of friction between members of the ship's company, all went smoothly for the *Hopeful Enterprise*. But on the morning of the tenth day the first hint of a change came up. It was a small hint, and could not have been described exactly as a warning of trouble, since it was something that was to be expected in that part of the ocean at that time of year. It was in fact a weather report picked up by Mr. Scotton, the radio officer, and it told of deteriorating conditions to the west moving rapidly eastward.

Scotton took the report to Captain Barling, and Barling read it through impassively. It was nothing to worry about. The bad weather would almost certainly catch up with them, and life on board ship would be rather less comfortable as a result, but it would probably not last long, and in a few days at the most they would be in port, this last voyage ended, finished; everything finished. Bad weather was a very minor problem.

" Thank you," Barling said.

Scotton left him and went back to the radio cabin, reflecting that Barling seemed to have aged a lot in the past few weeks. He wondered whether the Old Man was ill. Perhaps he had an ulcer. Scotton thought about it for a while and then forgot it. It was not really his concern.

It was an hour later when he came up with another signal, and this one was considerably more interesting: it was in fact the first Mayday call that Scotton had ever intercepted.

Barling was on the bridge with the third mate, a rather colourless young man named Stephen Walpole. Scotton was fairly bubbling over with excitement at the news he was bearing. A freighter called the *India Star* had sustained considerable damage from an explosion in the engine-room and was asking for assistance. The position given by the *India Star* put her about two hundred and fifty miles to the southwest of the *Hopeful Enterprise*.

Captain Barling read the signal, and he remembered afterwards the faint tingling sensation that came over him; he remembered it as the first intimation that here was something of importance, something that might affect him profoundly, even though as yet there was no more than the smallest hint of why or how; indeed, scarcely so much as a hint, but rather some inexplicable tremor of the nerves, a vibration, a vague stirring at the back of the mind.

" Any other ships answering the call?"

" There's a Panamanian tanker, the *Sargasso Queen*, about fifty miles south of her. They expect to close with her in three to four hours."

" Any others?"

" None closer than us, sir. At least, none answering."

Barling looked out through the wheelhouse window. The sky was overcast and there had been a little rain. The decks were wet and the tarpaulins on the hatches were stretched tight. He stared musingly at the bows of the ship cleaving through the water in a wash of foam, and he was thinking. Two hundred and fifty miles in the wrong direction. With the *Sargasso Queen* already on the way, was there any need to go? The *Hopeful Enterprise* could not hope to reach the stricken ship before the following day, and by that time all that was necessary would almost certainly have been done. It would be a wasted journey.

And yet, would it? Again that tingling of the nerves, that feeling that there was something here, something of importance, something not to be ignored. Call it a hunch. Besides, was it not his duty to answer the call, even though another ship was ahead of him? The *Sargasso Queen* might break down, might never reach the *India Star*; at sea nothing could be taken for granted.

He turned away from the window. " Make a signal to the *India Star* that we are on our way."

" Yes, sir," Scotton answered with enthusiasm, and went away like a winged Mercury.

Barling addressed the third mate. " Come into the chartroom. We've got a new course to plot."

Loder, when he became aware of the alteration in the ship's course and the reason for it, received the news with slightly cynical amusement. So Barling was off on an errand of mercy, was he? And an errand which was likely to prove quite unnecessary. Well, let him have his last fling, let him play the game out to the end if that was what he wanted. Loder, for his part, took a detached view of the entire business. His future did not lie with the *Hopeful Enterprise,* and already he was making his own plans.

Jonah Madden was again worrying about the engines. Barling had called for all possible speed, and it was not going to do them any good to stretch them to the limit. They needed nursing, and instead they were getting a hammering.

" It's just asking for trouble," he complained to Barling.

But Barling refused to listen. He had that hunch, and Madden could have as many qualms as he liked, it was not going to make any difference.

" There's a ship in distress, Chief."

Madden was gloomy. " We may be in distress ourselves before the night's out."

To Charlie Wilson it was a reprieve; it meant that a few extra days must pass before that inevitable arrest, and even though those days might be spent in purgatory he clutched at them none the less eagerly for that. Perhaps some miracle would happen to get him off the hook.

The rest of the crew on the whole accepted the situation with indifference, though a few of the younger men were mildly excited.

To Trubshaw it meant simply money. " More days, more dollars. It'll 'elp pay that fine. Wotcher say, Aussie?"

Lawson agreed. " Suits me. What's this *India Star* carrying?"

" Machinery, so I 'eard."

" She could sink easy then."

" She could sink afore we even get near 'er. Depends 'ow bad the damage is."

" Maybe we'll be getting passengers."

" Not likely," Trubshaw said. " By the time we get there in this old crate they'll all 'ave bin took off. Always supposin' they decide to abandon 'er, which ain't by any means certain."

During the day more information concerning the *India Star* was picked up by Scotton and gradually made its way, sometimes in rather garbled form, round the ship. It appeared that the explosion had been very severe; three men had been killed and two others injured; a fire had started, and the vessel had developed a slight list. The *Sargasso Queen* was making about fifteen knots and could be expected to arrive on the scene well before nightfall. Two other ships had answered the distress signal, but they were more than a day's steaming away. For all practical purposes, and barring accidents, the *Sargasso Queen* had the rescue operation to herself.

" We're wasting our time," Loder remarked to Madden. " You're straining your engines just for the Old Man's whim. We might as well turn about and head for home."

" You think so?" Madden's troubled eyes searched Loder's face. " You really think that?"

" It stands to reason," Loder said.

But Barling was not going by reason. There was that hunch. He continued to press Madden for all possible speed, ignoring all the chief engineer's prophecies of mechanical doom. The *Hopeful Enterprise* continued on her southwesterly course and the weather became progressively worse.

In the middle of the afternoon news came through that the *Sargasso Queen* had reached the *India Star* and was taking off all survivors. The two other ships that had been heading for the scene of the disaster concluded that their help would not be needed and reported that they were resuming their normal courses. Everyone on board the *Hopeful*

Enterprise, on hearing this news, assumed that their ship would do the same. Indeed, Mr. Thompson, the second mate, who was on watch at the time, took it so much for granted that he merely consulted Barling as a matter of form.

" You'll be calling it off now, sir?"

" No," Barling said. " Not yet."

Mr. Thompson was a stolid, thoroughly unimaginative man who took things much as they came and seldom showed the least trace of surprise even at the most unusual occurrence. In this instance, however, he made an exception, and his eyebrows, which in normal circumstances might have been regarded almost as fixtures, rose just a shade.

" Not yet?"

" That is what I said."

Mr. Thompson wished to get it quite clear in his mind so that there could be no possibility of a mistake. " You mean we are to continue on the same course, sir?"

" That is so. Have you any objection?"

" No," Thompson said. " I've no objection."

" Very well then."

Barling went down from the bridge and left Mr. Thompson to puzzle over this strange decision on the part of his captain. He had still found no adequate solution to the mystery when the mate relieved him for the first dog watch. Mr. Loder listened with an enigmatic expression as Thompson informed him that they were still on the same course, still heading in the direction of the crippled *India Star,* even though all the survivors had been taken on board the *Sargasso Queen.*

" I don't understand it," Thompson concluded. " Where's the point?"

" Perhaps you ought to ask the Old Man that."

" I could save my breath. Don't you have any theory?"

If Loder had, he was not disclosing it. " Ours not to reason why, Tommy. If that's how the man wants it, that's the way it's got to be."

" It's damned funny all the same."

" Well then, let's just have our laugh, shall we?"

Thompson stared at Loder and took note of the faint smile twisting the mate's thin lips. He had no more idea of what was passing in Loder's mind than he had of what was in Barling's. Sometimes he suspected that both of them were just a little way round the bend. And that was putting it mildly. But it was no business of his.

As he left the bridge he noticed that the wind was strengthening. The glass was beginning to fall.

An hour later Scotton picked up another signal from the *Sargasso Queen* to the effect that she was leaving the *India Star* and proceeding with all speed towards Southampton. One of the injured men was in a critical condition and needed to be taken to hospital with the least possible delay.

Barling questioned Scotton closely. " Any report on the condition of the *India Star*?"

" Only that she's afloat and that the fire is still burning, sir."

" I see."

Scotton looked at Barling, puzzled as much as Thompson had been. " We're still going there?"

" Yes," Barling said, " we're still going there."

" I don't understand, sir. There's nothing we can do now."

" Isn't there? Well, let's just say I'm curious. Now that we've come so far I'd hate not to take a look at the ship."

It sounded crazy to Scotton, but he did not say so. Another hundred and fifty miles or so of steaming, with the weather getting worse, just to see a derelict ship. It simply didn't make sense.

" We should be there early tomorrow," Barling said; and Scotton noticed that he sounded quite cheerful, as though he were only with difficulty suppressing wild excitement. " Oh, and Sparks, there is no need to report our position. For the present, in fact, I think it would be best if we maintained complete radio silence. You understand?"

" Yes, sir," Scotton said, and failed to understand in the least.

Throughout the night the *Hopeful Enterprise* steamed steadily towards the last reported position of the *India Star*. Barling was no longer pressing Madden to get the last ounce of power out of the engines; now that the survivors had been taken off there was not the same urgency. Nevertheless, he slept little; that scarcely repressed excitement kept him wakeful, and he made frequent visits to the bridge to confer with the officer of the watch. He could hardly wait for morning to come, for daylight would reveal whether or not he had committed himself and his ship to nothing more than a wild goose chase.

The first hints of dawn came in the mate's watch: a pale, cold light creeping up from the eastern horizon and revealing a slate-grey sea touched here and there with splashes of white where the wind flicked the wave-crests into spume. The *Hopeful Enterprise* was rolling a little, and Mr. Loder, peering through the wheelhouse window, could see the foremast swaying first to one side and then the other. A few feet away from him Able Seaman Trubshaw stood with his hands on the wheel, staring fixedly at the glowing binnacle, and with long-acquired skill keeping the ship on the desired course.

Trubshaw was wearing a blue jersey, a donkey-jacket and a cloth cap; he did not look particularly seamanlike; indeed, he could have passed equally well for a workman on a building site or a road-making project; but appearances were immaterial; it was the skill that counted, and Trubshaw had that.

He did not usually think much; he could do his trick at the wheel like an automaton, translating any orders given by the officer of the watch into the appropriate action as blindly, unquestioningly and accurately as any robot. When he thought at all it was usually to wonder what the cook was dishing up for breakfast or to anticipate the pleasures that awaited him when he stepped ashore in the next port of call.

On this particular morning, however, he allowed his mind to dwell on a different subject, and that subject was the carpenter, Sam Orwell. He had a score to settle with Orwell, and he intended to settle it before the ship reached England. Orwell could not be allowed to get away with what he had done, and Trubshaw meant to see that he did not get away with it. So he thought about the matter and came up with an idea, and the idea pleased him so much that he gave an involuntary chuckle.

Mr. Loder, hearing the chuckle, glanced at Trubshaw in some surprise; but Trubshaw's face in the dim light was hard and expressionless, and Loder concluded that perhaps he had been mistaken. What, after all, could there possibly be in this dreary morning scene to amuse any man?

A few moments later Barling came into the wheelhouse. Loder could sense the tension in Barling; it was apparent in the timbre of his voice.

" Anything to report?"

" Nothing," Loder said. He watched Barling move close up to the wheelhouse window and peer ahead into the greyness. " If you're looking for the *India Star* you'll need good eyesight. We've a way to go yet."

" I am aware of that," Barling answered with a touch of asperity.

" She could have sunk by now anyway."

Barling glanced at him sharply. " I believe you hope she has."

" Why should I hope that? How would it help me?"

Barling did not answer; he had no desire to be drawn into a pointless argument with the mate. Whether Loder hoped or did not hope that the *India Star* had sunk was of no importance; all that mattered was the fact, and there were still some hours to pass before the fact could be established one way or the other.

" Swine of a morning," Loder said.

Barling grunted.

" And it'll get worse."

Barling did not need to be told that. The weather could be the joker in the pack; it could make the whole idea even more fantastic than it already was. And when he thought about it he had to admit that it was fantastic. Yet if, against all probability, it could be brought off, what a reward there would be. For such a reward it was worth taking a chance, worth going two hundred and fifty miles off course, worth being suspected of having taken leave of his senses. Oh, yes, if he could bring it off it would be worth everything.

But the *India Star* had to be still afloat. If she had sunk there would be nothing; nothing but wasted miles of steaming in pursuit of a vain hope. She must be afloat.

He stood with his feet exactly fifteen inches apart, leaning against the slope of the deck as the ship rolled, perfectly balanced, scarcely aware of the movement, thinking of the prize that might perhaps be his.

It was in the forenoon watch, and the third mate was the first to catch sight of it. Captain Barling was again on the bridge and Mr. Walpole drew his attention.

" There, sir. Can you see it?"

It was fine on the port bow, a thin cloud of smoke away in the distance. Barling raised his binoculars to his eyes, adjusted the focus, and felt his heart leap. He went out of the wheelhouse on to the port wing of the bridge and looked again. The sky was overcast and visibility was poor, but he knew that he was seeing what he had come so far to see. Under that cloud of smoke was the *India Star*, still burning, but still afloat.

The prize was there.

SEVEN

INDIA STAR

SHE WAS there in the grey light of morning, drifting, abandoned, helpless, smoke rising from her amidships to be caught by the wind, blown away and dispersed. She was listing a few degrees to starboard, and the starboard davits had been swung out and the blocks were hanging loose where the boats had left them.

It must have been quite an explosion, for it had blown a hole clean through the superstructure above the boiler-room and had knocked the funnel over on to the boat-deck, where it was now lying like a stranded whale. A lot of the paint was blackened by smoke, but there was no sign of any flame and none of the woodwork appeared to be burnt, so it looked as though the fire must be confined to the boiler-room and engine-room.

Every man aboard the *Hopeful Enterprise* was on deck to look at her except those whose duties kept them below. She was an object of interest to all, though as yet no one but Captain Barling knew the purpose for which they were there.

There was something faintly eerie about that deserted ship with the smoke drifting from her; no one on her bridge, no look-out, no helmsman. Had they left the dead men in her? Were they the ship's company now?

" D'you think the rats 'ave left 'er?" Trubshaw said; but no one answered; no one laughed. It was not a joke.

The *Hopeful Enterprise* manoeuvred into a position a short distance to windward of the *India Star* and hove to. Scuds of rain were blowing across the decks, making conditions cold and unpleasant. Between the two ships the sea looked choppy and inhospitable. Loder, who had been called to the bridge by Captain Barling and was standing with him on the starboard wing, felt a trickle of ice-cold water running down his back.

" Well," he said, " we've found what we were looking for. Do we go home now?"

" You don't really think we came just for the view," Barling said. " It would hardly have been worth the trouble."

" If you came to rescue anyone, that was a waste of time. You can see there's no one left on board. The *Sargasso Queen* took the lot. What else is there?"

" There's a ship."

Loder stared at Barling in disbelief, and yet with a dawning realisation. " You can't be thinking of that."

" Of what?" Barling asked.

" Salvage."

Barling stroked his chin and gazed across at the *India Star* rolling in the swell. " And why not?"

" You mean to take that derelict in tow? With this?" Loder still could not believe it. " It's nearly a thousand miles. We'd never make it, not with our engines, and the weather. It's a mad idea."

" It's worth a try. That ship is carrying a valuable cargo."

" That ship could sink. She's still on fire."

Barling looked at the smoke coming from the *India Star*. " Not badly, I think. I'd say the fire is burning itself out."

Loder saw how it was: Barling was snatching at a straw. If he could bring this off the salvage money would save him. Loder had no doubt now that Barling was in severe financial straits; only a man with nothing to lose and all to gain would even consider such a desperate venture. The odds were heavily against him; they were beyond all reason. And yet there was just the faintest possibility that it might come off. In spite of himself Loder felt a flicker of excitement at the prospect.

But again he said: " It's a mad idea."

" Sometimes," Barling said, " a man needs to have a little madness."

" A thousand miles with that," Loder muttered; but there was a subtle change in his tone; it no longer sounded as though he were dismissing the idea as an impossibility but accepting it as a challenge. " A thousand miles with that on our tail."

" It would be something to talk about."

Loder shot a meaning glance at Barling. " It would be a lot more than that."

Barling saw that Loder understood. He looked for the cynicism in Loder's smile, but strangely, it was not there. The mate actually appeared to be eager to get on with the job.

" You'll see to the fixing of the tow. There's no point in delaying the operation."

" I'll do that," Loder said crisply. " I'll see to it at once."

There were four seamen in the boat—all volunteers. Charlie Wilson was one of them; it was something to take his mind off that other matter. And what if there was a touch of danger, a possibility of the boat's capsizing? To be drowned might be the best thing.

Sam Orwell, the carpenter, was also in the boat, and the others were Lawson, the Australian, and a Liverpool man named Veevers. Mr. Loder himself was at the helm.

It was the motor lifeboat and it was launched on the leeward side of the *Hopeful Enterprise*. It was no easy launch, for there was now a considerable sea running, and as the falls were paid out the ship rolled to starboard, sending the boat down fast towards the water, which smacked hard against the bottom and thrust it up again. As the falls slackened Orwell in the bows and Lawson in the stern released the hooks, and Wilson, aided by Veevers, thrust off from the ship's side with a boat-hook. The engine revved, the propeller churned, Loder pushed the helm over and the boat's bows lifted on a wave until it seemed that it would stand on end and topple back against the ship's plates. But the propeller thrust it forward and it rode up the wave, tilted on the crest and then went rushing down the other side.

The sea, viewed from the level of the boat, looked very different from the picture it presented when seen from the deck of the ship; the waves were so much higher, the troughs deeper. Even to a veteran seaman like Orwell it could seem a fearsome place and the life-jacket a comforting item of equipment.

Loder, peering through the flying spray, caught a glimpse of the *India Star* with smoke still rising from her, and he brought the boat's head round until they were making straight for the derelict ship. A thin line, secured to the stern of the lifeboat, was carefully paid out from a coil on the poop of the *Hopeful Enterprise* under the watchful eye of Bosun Rankin and the additional, if superfluous, supervision of the third mate.

Captain Barling, watching from the bridge in company with the second mate, could see the lifeboat tossing in the gulf between the two ships, thrown up high one moment, the next apparently swallowed up by the very element to which it had been entrusted.

" Think they'll make it, sir?" Thompson asked.

Barling answered rather testily: " Of course they'll make it. Why shouldn't they?"

" It's a nasty sea."

" Not as nasty as all that. What do you think lifeboats are built for?"

Thompson, seeing that Barling was a little edgy, decided to hold his tongue. It was no time for idle chatter. There was one thing though: he was glad it was Mr. Loder in that boat and not him. Loder was welcome to it.

A moment later Scotton appeared with an item of news.

" There's a tug on its way, sir."

Barling's head swivelled round. " What do you mean—a tug on its way?"

" It was a news flash on the radio, sir. There's a salvage tug coming out to look for the *India Star*. If she's still afloat it's going to take her in tow."

" Like hell it is," Barling said.

" You mean you're not going to wait for it, sir?" Scotton sounded surprised.

" Well, what do you think, Sparks? You're an intelligent young man. Do you imagine we came all this way to keep an eye on things for a salvage tug? No, Mr. Scotton; when the tug gets here the bird will have flown."

Scotton began to understand. " That's why you told me not to transmit any signals about our position?"

" Naturally," Barling said. " I thought you would have guessed that. No point in helping the opposition, is there?"

" I suppose not, sir," Scotton said, aghast at the audacity of the Old Man.

" However, there's no reason why you shouldn't keep an ear open for any signals they may make."

Scotton grinned suddenly. Barling was a cunning devil. He would never get away with it, of course; the *Hopeful Enterprise* would never haul that derelict all the way to England, not in a thousand years; but you had to give Barling full marks for trying.

" Yes, sir," he said, " I'll keep my ears open." He began to walk away.

" Incidentally," Barling said, " did they mention the name of that tug?"

Scotton turned. " Yes, sir. It's the *Atlantic Scavenger.*"

Barling smiled faintly. " This is one piece of garbage she's not going to scavenge."

The lifeboat was having a rough ride. Cold, drenching spray cascaded over it, and now and then water slopped over the gunwale and poured into the bottom. Loder, with the tiller under his arm, guided the boat with a skill born of years of experience. If he had felt inclined to cast his mind back he could have remembered a voyage in just such a boat thirty-five years ago, when he had been a young apprentice; a long and bitter voyage, with the survivors from a torpedoed ship dying one by one, from wounds, from privation, from a lack of the will to live. Loder had had that will; he and three others had endured ninety-six days in an open boat in the South Atlantic before reaching the coast of Brazil.

That experience had done something to Adam Loder; it had hardened him, dragged him viciously out of boyhood and made him a man, a man with no more illusions regarding human nature. He had seen how men could behave in the last extremity, and it had not been pleasant. He had seen murder committed for a few drops of fresh water, and it had seared his mind. There had been times when he had had nightmares in which he was back in that boat of death, but he never dreamed of it now, seldom even thought of it. It was past, as dead as those men who had been rolled overboard one by one.

The towering side of the *India Star* loomed up ahead of them. There was a Jacob's-ladder hanging down from the bulwarks just forward of the bridge, and amidships the dangling davit falls with the pulley-blocks and empty hooks oscillated like erratic pendulums, crashing against the steel hull with a startling clatter and then swinging away again.

"Stand by with the fenders," Loder said. "Starboard side."

The fenders, like rope puddings, were hung over the gunwale and Loder steered the boat towards the Jacob's-ladder, bringing it broadside on, then cutting the engine and letting it drift against the ship's side. A wave lifted it, hurled it sideways, and the fenders were crushed between timber and steel, squeaking under the pressure. Orwell and Lawson grabbed the ladder, and Mr. Loder, jumping quickly up from the sternsheets, was first to climb over the bulwark of the *India Star*. Looking down, he shouted to the carpenter to make the boat fast and to bring the line aboard.

"I'm going to take a look at the damage."

He was gone immediately, making for the ladder to the centre castle. Fifteen seconds later he was standing at the forward end of the boat-deck and surveying the scene of destruction. In front of him was a gaping hole, jagged at the edges, and from this hole a grey column of smoke was rising. The wind was blowing the smoke away from him, but he could smell it and taste it; it caught at his throat and nostrils, sulphurous and stinging.

The great open end of the funnel faced him across the gap, and the funnel itself was lying amid a tangle of crushed ventilators, crumpled stays and twisted stanchions. As the ship rolled the funnel seemed to be making spasmodic attempts to free itself, and it made a screeching sound, as though the effort were causing it the most exquisite agony.

Loder, taking extreme care on the moving deck, went down on hands and knees, then flat on his stomach, and dragged himself cautiously to the edge of the hole. Peering down into the heart of the ship, he could see nothing very clearly because of the smoke, but he had an impression of torn and twisted metal, of steel ladders wrenched into fantastic convolutions, and somewhere, far below, a dull red glow.

He was about to draw back when something else caught his eye. At first he did not believe it, but then the smoke in that particular area thinned momentarily and he could see that there had been no mistake: what he was gazing at, and what appeared to be gazing back at him, was indeed a man's head. Torn from its body, it had by some strange freak of the explosion been thrown almost to the level of the deck on which Loder was lying and there had become impaled on a steel rod that had originally perhaps been part of a handrail.

For possibly half a minute Loder gazed down at this blackened and bloody relic which had so recently been part of a living man; then the smoke swirled up more thickly and he drew back, choking. He crawled away from the hole, got to his feet and returned to the foredeck.

The men were waiting for him expectantly.

" Well, sir?" Orwell said, not putting the question in more precise form.

Loder understood him. " There's a chance. It seems to be a slow fire. We'd better get the tow-rope across."

They had already brought the line up from the boat. Now they moved to the forecastle, taking the line with them. Standing near the bows, Loder gazed across at the *Hopeful Enterprise* some two hundred yards distant. Using his arms as a semaphore, he made a brief signal and got an equally brief acknowledgement from the poop of the other ship.

"Haul away then."

The men began hauling in the line and then felt the increasing weight of the heavier messenger rope that had been bent to the other end. When the messenger came up over the bows the weight became even greater; there was now a wire hawser attached to it.

Orwell chanted the rhythm in his thick, gruff voice: "Altogether—heave! And again—heave!"

The rope came in, dripping with salt water, and Loder also lent a hand. It was hard, skin-rasping, back-breaking work, but they kept at it, panting with exertion, bringing the rope foot by foot through the fairlead and dragging the submerged hawser slowly but surely across the gap.

At last, after nearly fifteen minutes of steady hauling, the eye of the hawser broke the surface.

"Now, lads—hup! And once more—hup!"

They had it now. The eye came up through the fairlead, the wire rope shining with grease and sea-water. They belayed the hawser to a pair of bollards and shackled the eye to a deck clench. After that they were able to relax and get their breath back, easing their aching muscles.

But there was no time to waste. Loder was anxious to get back to the *Hopeful Enterprise*. His task here was completed and he had no wish to stay on board the derelict any longer than was necessary. The fire might not appear to be serious, but there was no telling with such things; it might flare up suddenly, or there might be another explosion. If anything of that kind happened he would rather be well away from it.

" All right, men. Back to the boat."

The lifeboat had been bumping against the side of the ship but had been saved from damage by the fenders. A quantity of water had got into it and the bottom boards were awash. On the return trip they were able to occupy themselves with baling.

Captain Barling was pleased. So far everything had gone smoothly. And Loder's report that the fire in the *India Star* showed no immediate signs of flaring up was good news.

" What is your estimation of the chances of her staying afloat now that you've had a look?"

Loder was reluctant to commit himself. " Difficult to say. A lot will depend on the weather. She doesn't appear to be holed anywhere, though there could be damage below the waterline. There's that list too. It's not bad at present, but it could get worse. Some of the cargo may have shifted."

" You're looking on the black side."

" No point in blinding oneself to the possibilities. Conditions aren't improving."

There could be no doubt about that; they had got appreciably worse even in the time it had taken to fix the tow-rope, and the trip back to the *Hopeful Enterprise* had been even more hazardous than the outward one. None of the men in the boat had been at all sorry to see the hooks latched on again and the falls being drawn in. They felt a great deal safer standing again on the solid steel deck, even if that deck was beginning to imitate the motion of a seesaw.

The *Hopeful Enterprise* went ahead slowly, taking up the

slack in the tow-rope. Three hundred yards astern the bows of the *India Star* dipped as though acknowledging a new master. The long tow had begun.

EIGHT

NOT IMPORTANT

THEY SETTLED down to a speed of about three knots, and
the rain fell steadily from a leaden sky, the wind driving it
across the decks to mingle with the salt spray tossed up
from the sea. The ship ahead and the ship astern both rolled,
sometimes in unison, sometimes not, so that the masts of the
Hopeful Enterprise might be leaning over to starboard
while those of the *India Star* leaned to port. At times the
India Star was almost lost from sight in the murk; at best
she was no more than an ill-defined mass rising out of the
water.

It was difficult to realise just how highly valuable
that shadowy mass might be. If only it would stay afloat long
enough; if only the fire would stay within bounds; if only the
list would not get worse; if only the *Hopeful Enterprise*
could keep going.

" We'll never do it, you know," Trubshaw said. " The Old
Man's crazy even to think abaht it. Christ, 'e wants 'is brains
tested."

Lawson disagreed. He had helped to get the tow-rope
across and he felt a kind of proprietorial interest in the
operation. " We'll make it. You're too bloody pessimistic,
chum."

" Pessimistic? Nah. What's it ter me? I don't stand t'git

nothin' aht of it. The Old Man, yes. But what's in it for you an' me, mate? That's what I'd like t'know."

" We'll get our share."

" 'Owja know that?" Trubshaw stabbed a thick, inquisitorial finger into Lawson's chest. " Is that the law?"

" I don't know about the law. But the Old Man'll see us right."

Trubshaw gave a jeering laugh. " I reckon you believe in Father Christmas too. You mark my words, the Old Man'll grab all 'e can; 'e won't care a damn abaht us. That's 'is prize aht there, not ours."

The table in the seamen's messroom tilted as the ship rolled heavily; the door swung open and slammed shut again; above the rattling and creaking they could hear the sea beating against the hull and the wind howling.

Moir said: " The only one that's going to get that prize is Mr. Davy Jones."

" We'll make it," Lawson said again.

Trubshaw laughed and began to roll a cigarette.

Night had fallen. There was a powerful spotlight fixed to the taffrail of the *Hopeful Enterprise* and there was a seaman keeping watch on the towing hawser. In the beam of the spotlight he caught an occasional glimpse of the *India Star* plunging along at the end of the tow.

The seaman was able to get a little shelter from the wind and the rain by huddling against the lee side of the poop deckhouse, but with the deck lifting and falling and shuddering it was at best an uncomfortable post to say the least. From time to time he could hear the rattle of the steering machinery and the sudden crack of spray hitting the other side of the deckhouse like the flick of a whip. He pulled the collar of his oilskin coat more closely about his neck and waited morosely for the hours of his watch to pass.

The night wore away and morning came, and the *India Star* was still there, still with the thin banner of smoke trailing from her, still with the same slight list to starboard. Barling, early on the bridge after a few hours' sleep, observed her with satisfaction, studying her through his binoculars.

" We're doing well," he remarked to the mate. " Very well indeed."

Mr. Loder had had a tedious four-hour watch and was not in the most cheerful of moods. " There's a long way to go yet."

Barling felt a stab of annoyance with Loder; he did not want anyone pouring cold water on his hopes. He answered a little sharply: " I know there's a long way to go. That doesn't alter the fact that we're doing well."

" It doesn't alter anything," Loder said.

Indeed, nothing had altered: the weather was as it had been at nightfall; the wind blowing gustily from the southwest, the sky overcast, rain falling, the sea rough. Conditions were neither better nor worse.

They were some fifty miles nearer home.

" Is Madden happy?" Loder asked.

" Madden is never happy. It's contrary to his nature. But I believe he's reasonably satisfied with the way the engines have behaved so far. More than that can hardly be expected from him."

Loder had it on the tip of his tongue to repeat his earlier observation that there was a long way still to go, but he thought better of it. He had, in the grey disillusion of the morning watch, lost much of that uncharacteristic enthusiasm which had come over him the previous day when the job of fixing the towing hawser had to be taken in hand. Now he remembered the impaled head that he had seen through the smoke and he felt depressed. Where was the point of all this striving if that was what it finally came to? Here was George Barling pinning all his hopes to an operation that had no real chance of success, and to what end? A few more years and he would be dead anyway, snuffed out as completely as those men who had been caught by the explosion in the *India Star*. Life! It was nothing; just a lot of trouble leading to extinction. The hell with it.

This kind of mood of utter nihilism was not unusual with Loder during the last part of a watch that began at four in the morning and continued until eight. And it was especially in evidence when the dawn came cold and grey and wet like an old army blanket soaked in water. He would feel better when he had got some food inside him. No man could be expected to be at his best before breakfast.

Barling was not concerned with Loder's mood. He looked again at the *India Star*, the prize that had somehow to be towed those hundreds of miles to safety. For Ann's sake it had to be done.

A few hours later Scotton brought news. He had picked up signals from the *Atlantic Scavenger*. The tug was still heading westwards at full speed and expected to be in the vicinity of the *India Star* in about two more days.

" Making good time," Barling commented. " I've no doubt she can manage fifteen knots. Well, she'll find the cupboard bare."

"You don't think we ought to let them know, sir?" Scotton sounded a little worried. " I mean, it's wasting their time. And they couldn't take the *India Star* away from us, could they? She's ours by right now, isn't she?"

" Yes, she's ours by right."

" Then why the secrecy, sir?"

Barling had no convincing answer to that. There was no good reason why it should not be made known that they had taken the derelict in tow. As Scotton had said, the *Atlantic Scavenger* could not take it away from them. Nevertheless, he had a feeling, unreasonable as it might be, that to broadcast the information would be in some way to put the prize in jeopardy, to tempt fate to snatch it from him. No; the fewer people who knew about it, the better; and as long as Scotton kept his radio silent no one outside the *Hopeful Enterprise* could know.

"Never mind why," he said. "Just carry out orders."

"Yes, sir," Scotton said, and felt resentful. He had been snubbed and did not like it. "Is there anything else?"

"Anything new on the weather?"

"Nothing good, sir. It seems likely to get worse."

Barling did not care for the sound of that, but he was not surprised. Scotton's words merely supported his own deductions. The glass was still falling.

"Well," he said, "we shall just have to make the best of it."

All day the *Hopeful Enterprise* plodded on at the same depressingly low speed. It was scarcely walking pace, and it irked Barling. He would dearly have liked to go faster, but he knew that to press for more knots would be to risk everything. One had to have patience. Yet patience, in the face of this mounting threat from the weather, was difficult to maintain.

He consulted with Madden. An extra knot perhaps? Madden opposed the suggestion with every argument at his command, and Barling knew that in this instance the chief engineer was right.

"Very well, then. We'll leave things as they are."

" I only hope and pray they stay like it."

Madden looked tired and worried, even haggard. Barling remarked on it.

" You're not looking well. I think you ought to get some sleep."

" Sleep! " Madden sounded shocked. Barling might have been suggesting a shot of heroin to judge by his reaction. " I can't sleep."

" If you don't get some rest it's you that'll have the breakdown, not the engines. You don't have to watch them all the time."

" That's what you think," Madden said darkly, and went away rubbing his nose and looking like a small local depression.

By nightfall they had been towing for nearly thirty hours and had lopped almost a hundred miles off the distance that had to be covered. But Captain Barling felt no inclination to complacency; if there had been no other reason, the weather would have been sufficient to dispel any such feeling. For it had appreciably worsened. The wind, backing a little, was now hitting them more on the beam and with much increased strength, building up the sea and causing the *Hopeful Enterprise* and her helpless consort to roll more and more heavily.

The smoke, still coming from the *India Star*, scarcely rose at all; as soon as it emerged from the hole in her decks it was pounced on by the wind, flattened out and carried away just above the crests of the waves. The whole vast circle of water, as far as the eye could see, was nothing but hills and valleys, streaked with white, spume blowing from the peaks like smoke, paler but thicker than that which issued from the crippled ship.

The *India Star*, straining at the leash, plunging and yawing seemed intent on breaking free; and Charlie Wilson, doing his stint of tow-rope watch in the late afternoon, could hear the hawser screeching as it rubbed against the sides of the fairlead. Now and then he thought he detected a kind of twanging sound, like a distant harp, but the wind was making so much noise anyway that he could not be certain. The poop was becoming more and more inhospitable as the sea grew more boisterous. The stern rose and fell with a sickening motion, and as it fell a monstrous hill of water appeared to be tossed up beyond the taffrail, blocking out all view of the *India Star* and threatening, so it seemed, to engulf the entire after part of the *Hopeful Enterprise*.

Wilson stared at the *India Star* whenever she became visible and wondered how much longer she would stay afloat. And he wondered what he ought to do if suddenly she was no longer there. Suppose she went down so quickly that there was no time to release the hawser. Would she drag the *Hopeful Enterprise* down with her?

He put this question to Sandy Moir when the Scotsman came to relieve him, but Moir was unworried.

" Ye can put that oot of your mind, laddie. It'll tak' more than a wire-rope to pull this old girl doon. Yon hawser would part under the strain."

Wilson supposed Moir was right. After all, the ship was able to carry thousands of tons of cargo without being forced under, and the breaking strength of the hawser could not be more than two or three tons—a negligible addition to the load.

" Do you think we're going to get that ship safely to port?"

Moir gave a derisive laugh. " There's never a snowball's chance in hell o' that. If it was me making the decisions we'd be slipping that tow-rope right this very minute and calling it a day."

"Ah, but it's not you making the decisions, is it?" Wilson said, and he left Moir to find what shelter he could in the lee of the deckhouse.

It was six o'clock in the morning when Trubshaw took over from Veevers on tow-rope watch. It had been a wild night and it was still pitch dark, the lamp on the stern throwing the waves into startling relief and shining on the dripping hawser.

"The bastard's still there then," Trubshaw said.

Veevers grunted. "It's a bleedin' miracle, that's what it is. I'd've said she'd be gone long ago."

"Which goes to show you ain't no prophet."

"Maybe the Old Man's not so mad after all. Maybe he knows what he's doing."

"Give it time," Trubshaw said. He cocked his head on one side, listening. "What's that?"

"What's what?"

"Kinda 'ummin' sound."

"It's the hawser," Veevers said. "Makes that sound now and again. Like it was trying to play a tune."

"Ain't the sorta tune I like." Trubshaw seemed a shade uneasy. "You reported it?"

"Reported it? Why would I report a thing like that? Not important, is it?"

"S'pose not."

"Well, behave yourself, wack."

Veevers went away and left Trubshaw to his vigil. It was raining again, and the rain was being driven across the poop by the wind, which must have been getting near to gale force in the gusts. There was plenty of spray too;

Trubshaw could tell the rain from the spray by the taste; the spray was salty on his tongue. In a partial lull he again heard that humming sound. He wondered whether to ring the bridge and report it to the officer of the watch, but he remembered that it was the mate up there and he wanted none of Mr. Loder's sarcastic comments. He decided to let it go. It was probably, as Veevers had said, not important.

At a quarter-past six Sam Orwell awoke, reached for the butt of a cigarette that he had stubbed out before going to sleep, lit it, and lay for a while in his bunk, smoking and listening to the sounds of a ship under stress. Orwell coughed, the smoke from the cigarette butt getting on to his chest. He ignored the cough, went on smoking until his lips were in danger of being scorched, then crushed the remains of the tobacco and paper into a tin screwed to the bulkhead and heaved himself out of the bunk.

The small cabin was moving so erratically that dressing was no easy task. But Orwell accomplished it, and having dragged on gumboots, oilskin coat and sou'wester, he left the cabin and made his way out on deck.

He was driven by curiosity more than anything else, for it was no duty of his to turn out at that hour and inspect the tow. But he wanted to see for himself how things were going, whether the *India Star* was still with them or whether the two ships had parted company in the night.

The cold wind struck him as he clawed his way towards the stern, flicking rain and spray into his face, and with the deck behaving crazily under his feet, he was obliged to move carefully from one handhold to the next. He could see the powerful electric lamp cutting a swathe of light through the darkness astern, but no one appeared to be keeping watch on the tow-rope.

He gave a shout: "Hi, there! Anyone about?"

No one answered, and he shouted again, "Anyone here? Anyone on watch?"

He had reached the after end of the poop deckhouse and had still seen no one, and he was beginning to wonder a little uneasily whether some accident had occurred, whether perhaps the man who should have been on watch had been washed overboard. With this sea running it was not impossible. He moved to the taffrail, rested his hands on it and looked at the cauldron of water below him. If anyone had gone into that it was goodbye to him, that was for certain.

He was turning away from the rail when he heard Trubshaw's voice.

"Gotcher knife with you this time, Chippie?"

Trubshaw had come up behind him, and before he could make a move to defend himself Trubshaw's iron fist crashed into the side of his neck. It was like a club hitting him. He staggered under the impact, clutched at the rail for support, failed to make contact, lost his balance as the deck tilted, and fell heavily. He tried to get up, and Trubshaw slammed him down again with his foot, stamping viciously and grinding his heel into Orwell's ribs.

"Nobody pulls a knife on me an' gets away with it. I been watchin' you, Chippie. I been watchin' an' waitin'. Now I gotcher where I wancher, an' I'm really goin' t'make you pay for wadjew done."

He began to kick Orwell. Orwell rolled over and felt the stab of Trubshaw's toe in the small of his back. He stretched out his right arm and got one of the rails under his hand. He gripped it and pulled himself up. Trubshaw attempted to kick him again, but the movement of the deck took him off balance; he staggered and was saved from falling only by the wall of the deckhouse. By the time he had recovered

Orwell was on his feet, gasping and still slightly dazed, his back against the taffrail.

Trubshaw was angry; he rushed in again and swung his right fist at Orwell's jaw. Orwell saw the blow coming and instinctively shifted his head to the right. Trubshaw's fist slid past Orwell's left ear and the momentum carried him on so that the full weight of his body crashed into Orwell, driving the carpenter back against the rail. Trubshaw dropped both hands on to the taffrail, one on each side of Orwell, and held him pinned there, unable to break free.

" I gotcher now," he grunted. " You don't get away this time."

Orwell's arms were locked against his sides. He tried to bring his knee up but he was hampered by the long oilskin coat that he was wearing. Trubshaw was beginning to exert pressure, and Orwell could hear him panting, could smell the unpleasant odour of Trubshaw's breath.

" I'm goin' t'make you really squirm, Chippie. I'm goin' t'make you squeal, you bastard."

" Don't be a fool, Trub," Orwell said. " Give over."

Trubshaw gave a sneering laugh. " Beginnin' to 'urt, is it? Well, you squeal, just you squeal; then we'll see."

He increased the pressure, forcing Orwell back over the taffrail. Orwell was in real pain, and he wondered how much further Trubshaw would go if he did not squeal for mercy. It went against the grain to plead a favour from such a man, to admit defeat; but better that than a broken spine.

" All right, Trub, you win." He was gasping with the agony in his back. " Give over now. You got me licked."

Trubshaw laughed again but did not relax his grip. " Well, that's sumfin'. That's gettin' on the way. But it don't amount to squealin'. So squeal, you bastard, squeal."

" No," Orwell said. " Damned if I will. To hell with that."

And this time he managed to bring his knee up into Trub-shaw's stomach and heard the man grunt. It must have hurt Trubshaw, but it did not have the desired effect of making him release his grip. Just the opposite in fact, for it seemed merely to enrage him, and the pressure increased until it was scarcely bearable.

Orwell was bent back over the taffrail like a bow, and he knew that something had to break. He could hear the water churning past below him, and he wondered whether Trubshaw had so completely lost control of his temper that he really meant to kill him, to throw him overboard and let the sea take him. Orwell knew that it was only too probable; when Trubshaw was in a rage he just went berserk.

Despite himself, Orwell gave a cry of pain; the agony in his back was beyond all bearing. " Trub! For Christ's sake!"

He might have saved his breath. Trubshaw was past being appealed to, past reason. Orwell knew in that moment that he was going to die. And he knew that he was afraid of death.

It was a moment when the wind eased for an instant; a strange lull when the banshee howling dropped to a sob. In that momentary lull both men heard the other sound—the humming of the wire hawser. It seemed to get through to Trubshaw, through the wall of rage that encased him, to impinge on his consciousness. He turned his head to one side, listening, yet still not slackening the pressure.

Orwell listened too, and the humming noise rose in pitch, rose to a high, thin whine, almost like a human scream. And then there was a sudden crack, and there was no more humming or whining. But something came whipping back from the fairlead, something thin and sinuous like a striking snake; and it lashed Trubshaw across the back of the neck, tearing through the sou'wester and through the collar of his coat, tearing through to the flesh and tearing that too. And Trubshaw released Orwell, and flung his hands up to his neck and went staggering back, shrieking.

Orwell straightened his back, and all the vertebrae seemed to be crying out in protest. He hung on to the taffrail and heard Trubshaw screaming; and he looked at the fairlead and saw that there was no hawser passing through it now. But there was a length of wire rope lying on the deck, frayed at the end, and perhaps with some blood on it if it had been possible to see.

He turned his head slowly and looked down the pale corridor astern where the light was shining, and he caught a fleeting glimpse of the other ship. Then she was gone, swallowed up in the darkness, and he did not see her again.

NINE

NEVER SINGLY

" IT WAS bound to happen," Loder said. " In a sea like this there was too much strain. It wasn't even a new hawser."

He was talking to Madden in the saloon, drinking a well-earned cup of coffee and resting his legs. After a long watch in rough weather the legs got very tired; they were under stress the whole time; it was as bad as a cross-country run.

" I hear one of the seamen got caught by the back-lash from the hawser," Madden said. " Is it bad?"

" He'll live. It took a slice out of the back of his neck, but he was lucky: it could have blinded him. The carpenter happened to be standing by, which was another piece of luck for Trubshaw; Orwell was able to help him. The steward's looking after him now."

He drank some more coffee, warming both hands on the cup and feeling the warmth running down inside him.

Madden said: " I suppose now we make for home."

" No," Loder said.

" No?"

" Didn't you know? We're going to hunt for the lost sheep."

" The *India Star*?"

" None other."

" But we couldn't pick her up again in this." Madden

turned his head slightly, ear cocked to the sounds of the gale which penetrated to the interior of the ship. "Even if we found her, even if she isn't sunk, it just wouldn't be possible."

"Agreed. But the plan is to wait until the weather eases and then take her in tow again as soon as we find her. If we find her."

"It's impossible."

"Not impossible. Just crazy. Odds of a million to one against. But the Old Man's dead set on getting that ship." He drained his cup, took a small cigar from a case in his pocket and lit it. He tilted his head back and let smoke drift from his mouth. It put him in mind of the smoke coming from the hole in the decks of the *India Star*. He wondered whether that fire was still burning, or whether it had been quenched by the sea, swallowed up with the ship and the cargo. "And of course we all know why, don't we, Chief?"

"Do we?" Madden said.

Loder gave a laugh. "Oh, come off it, Chief. Don't pretend you don't know as well as I do that getting that salvage money is his last chance of saving the Company."

"Is that what you think?" Madden peered at Loder with his anxious, watery eyes.

"I wouldn't mind taking a bet on it."

"Yes," Madden said, thinking it over, "I suppose you could be right. If he is in difficulty—"

"Oh, he is. No doubt about it."

"If he is in difficulty, it would answer his problem. A ship like that, with the kind of cargo she's carrying, must be worth a fortune. It would solve everything." Madden's voice dropped almost to a whisper. "Everything."

"But it won't."

Madden's head jerked up, his eyes once again searching Loder's. "Why not?"

"Because we'll never take the ship in. Not now. If there ever was a chance—and it was a pretty slim one at best—it went west when that tow-rope parted. Now the chance isn't just slim: it doesn't exist."

"I suppose not." Madden sounded depressed.

"We may as well forget about it now."

Madden sighed heavily. "I suppose so."

But George Barling had not forgotten it. As long as there was one small fragment of hope remaining Barling would cling to it. Even if the odds were, as Loder had said, a million to one against him, Barling would not give up. He had seen salvation on the end of a tow-rope and he meant to see it there again if that were humanly possible.

He was well aware, nevertheless, that in the prevailing conditions it would be useless to search for the *India Star*. Even if they found her it would be quite impossible to get another hawser fixed. So the only thing to do was to hang about in the area until the gale abated, then make a search. The *India Star* would have drifted of course, but they could make a rough calculation of the likely direction and amount of the drift, and allow for it. He was aware that Loder thought it was a waste of time, but he was not interested in what Loder thought. The decision was for him to make, and he had made it. With her propeller turning over just fast enough to give steerage way, the *Hopeful Enterprise* turned her head to the wind and prepared to ride out the storm.

Trubshaw was in the hospital amidships. The hospital was a small, white-painted cabin with two bunks, and Trubshaw had it to himself. Orwell went along at mid-

morning smoko to see how he was getting on. He found
Trubshaw lying on his back with a lot of white bandage
swathed about his neck. There was a growth of stubble on
his face, but the skin looked pale, as though drained of
blood.

He did not turn his head when Orwell walked in; it was
doubtful whether he could have done so; but his eyes moved.
Orwell closed the door and crossed to the bunk.

" How are you feeling, Trub?"

Trubshaw looked up at him and did not answer at once;
and when he did speak it was in a voice so hoarse and weak,
it hardly seemed like his.

" I feel bloody terrible."

" You're lucky to be alive."

" Lucky?"

" And if it comes to that," Orwell continued, " I'm lucky
to be alive too. You'd have killed me, wouldn't you?"

The bunk was moving like a seesaw. Trubshaw groaned.
He seemed to be in pain.

" You would, wouldn't you?" Orwell said, hanging on to
the tubular iron framework and bringing his black-bearded
face closer to Trubshaw's. " That's the truth, isn't it? You'd
have pitched me overboard."

" No," Trubshaw said. " You can't pin that on me."

Orwell glanced towards the door and back at Trubshaw.
" Why trouble to deny it? There's only the two of us here.
And we both know."

" No."

" We both know you were so mad you'd have broke my
back and tipped me over the taffrail if that tow-rope hadn't
parted and given you a smack. That's what saved my life.
But it was no thanks to you."

" 'Ave you told anyone?"

" No, I haven't told anyone."

" Are you goin' to?"

" I've not made up my mind."

" Nobody'd believe you."

" People who know you would. People who know what a vicious bastard you are."

Trubshaw was silent, staring up at Orwell. Then he said: " You ain't goin' to tell nobody, Chippie."

" Maybe not," Orwell said. " But that's not to say it's all forgive and forget. I'm not a forgiving man, Trub." He remembered that moment when he had known he was going to die. He remembered being afraid. Trubshaw had made him afraid; it was easier to forgive the physical injury than that.

" So wotcher goin' to do abaht it?" There was a more truculent note in Trubshaw's hoarse voice now.

Orwell tugged reflectively at his beard. " Well, let's see. I might do summat right here and now. You're as helpless as a baby lying there. Suppose I was to slip a knife into you."

" You wouldn't do it," Trubshaw said; but he was not quite so truculent. He seemed uneasy. " You wouldn't get away with it."

" No reason why I shouldn't. Nobody knows I'm here. Nobody saw me come in. Nobody'll see me go out. I'd say there's plenty of others in this ship that wouldn't cry their eyes out if you snuffed it. Plenty of suspects, like in all the best detective yarns. No proof though. Think of that, Trub."

" You wouldn't do it," Trubshaw said again; he seemed to be trying to convince himself.

" No?" Orwell put his right hand behind his back and drew the knife from its pigskin sheath. He held it in front of Trubshaw's eyes. " You've seen this before."

Trubshaw stared at the knife and did not move. Orwell laid his right hand on Trubshaw's chest, holding the knife so that its point was just touching the soft underpart of Trubshaw's jaw where the bandage ended.

" I could press it in there and slit your throat. No trouble at all."

Trubshaw said nothing, still did not move. He looked at Orwell with fear growing in his eyes, and his hands lay motionless on the blanket that covered him. He did not attempt to raise them and grip Orwell's wrist, to try to wrest the knife from him; he seemed to know that it would have been useless. Orwell had merely to thrust once and the knife would be in his throat.

They remained thus for a full minute, staring into each other's eyes and not speaking a word. Then Orwell gave a laugh and put the knife back in its sheath. Trubshaw allowed his pent-up breath to escape with a hiss.

Orwell laughed again. " You thought I would do it, didn't you?"

" No."

" You're a bloody liar. I could see it in your eyes."

" So you're a mind-reader as well as a carpenter."

" I can see when a man's afraid. You were afraid."

Trubshaw did not continue with the argument. He appeared to be suffering. There were lines of pain around his mouth.

" But why should I trouble to kill you?" Orwell said. " You'll die anyroad. You'll be dead before we reach port."

" No. I'm not goin' to die."

" You don't look good to me."

" Of course I don't. I oughter be in 'ospital."

" The only hospital you'll see is this one. With the steward to look after you. And a lot he knows about doctoring.

That neck of yours could get gangrene, and then what?"

Trubshaw's eyes glared hatred at his tormentor, but there was apprehension in them too. There might be something in what Orwell was saying. After all, what did the steward know about medicine? It was not as if he was a qualified doctor.

" We'll be 'ome in a few days now. I'll get proper treatment then."

" Home! You can put that out of your head rightaway. It'll be weeks before we're home at the rate we're going."

" Wotcher mean? We ain't got that 'anger-on now. We oughter be makin' good time."

" I've got news for you," Orwell said. " We're waiting for this storm to die down, then we're going hunting."

" 'Untin'?"

" For the hanger-on that's not hanging on any more. And when we've found it we're going to take it in tow again. You won't be going ashore just yet."

" Christ!" Trubshaw said. " The Old Man must be bonkers."

Orwell grinned malevolently. " Oh, he is. But it's not going to do you any good, is it?" He walked to the door, then turned. " Think about it, Trub. Think about dying." He went out and closed the door behind him.

When Orwell had gone Trubshaw lay on his bunk and listened to the sounds of the ship: the creaking and groaning, the occasional clang of metal on metal, the thump of the engines. His neck hurt; it hurt like hell. Suppose Orwell was right. Suppose it did turn to gangrene. Suppose he were to die.

The idea of death frightened Trubshaw. It was all right when you were doing something active; he had never been scared of death in the wartime convoys; at least, if he had, he had forgotten it now. But that was different; that was not like this—lying helpless, waiting for death to come and take you. " Think about dying," Orwell had said. Trubshaw thought about it and felt sick. He was not old enough to die; he was hardly fifty; plenty of years in him yet, good years, in which to enjoy life, do things. But people died any time; nobody could guarantee you your full ration of life; so maybe the time had come for him. And what about after? Was there anything or nothing? Did you wake again like the preachers said, or were you just snuffed out like a candle? There was only one way of finding out for certain, and that was the way Trubshaw did not wish to take.

Thinking about dying, and hating the thought, Trubshaw incautiously turned his head and felt a stab of pain in his neck so fierce that he cried out with the agony of it. After that he lay very still, groaning a little, and wondering whether it was the gangrene beginning to bite.

If Sam Orwell had seen him then he would have been well satisfied with the results of his visit, very well satisfied.

The gale continued with no appreciable abatement. The *Hopeful Enterprise* faced it, her propeller revolving slowly and the seas breaking over her bows. Spray, caught by the wind, was flung up to the bridge and spattered against the windows of the wheelhouse; halyards, stretched to the limit, vibrated like harp strings, and wailing, as of a multitude of bereaved women, rose and fell in a dismal dirge of woe.

Scotton, limited by orders of his captain to listening only, caught occasional transmissions from the *Atlantic Scavenger*, which he carried to Barling.

" They're in the area where the *India Star* was last heard of, sir."

" But haven't sighted her?"

" No, sir. And in their last report they don't sound very hopeful. They think that in this sea the *India Star* has probably sunk."

Barling nodded thoughtfully. " Is that so?"

" Well, it is rather likely, sir," Scotton ventured to suggest.

Barling stared at him bleakly. " I do not accept that."

" No, sir."

" I refuse to accept it."

" Yes, sir." Scotton could see that Barling did not want to believe that the *India Star* had gone down, and any suggestion that she might have done so was not going to be received with any pleasure. He decided that his most prudent course would be to go along with Barling. " I suppose a ship like that could stay afloat in spite of the damage."

" The damage was all amidships. There is no reason at all why she shouldn't remain afloat."

" Of course not, sir."

" Have you got any more on the weather?"

" Rather more promising, sir." Scotton was glad to be able to report some good news. " The gales appear to be moving away eastward."

" Good. As soon as conditions have moderated sufficiently we shall start searching."

" Yes, sir," Scotton said, and refrained from adding what he thought—that it would be a vain search.

" Did you gather what the *Atlantic Scavenger* proposed doing?"

" Apparently they're going to cruise around for a time; but I don't think they'll keep it up long. Not from the way they spoke."

Barling hoped they would not. He did not want any competition from the tug when the weather cleared. It was fortunate that, before the tow-rope parted, the *India Star* had at least been moved some distance from the spot where she had been originally abandoned. That meant that the *Atlantic Scavenger* would be searching in the wrong area. It was just as well that he had had the foresight to impose strict radio silence, otherwise young Scotton might have given the whole show away.

All in all, he was feeling reasonably satisfied with the way things were going. Until the engines broke down.

Barling received the report from a gloomy Jonah Madden and could make very little of the engineer's jargon.

" Spare me all that. I just want to know one thing: can you and your bright lads fix it?"

Madden, interrupted in full flow, answered somewhat aggrievedly: " We can try."

" I know you can try. What I'm asking is, can you do it?"

" It may take time."

" How much time? An hour? Two hours?"

" More than that."

" But you can fix it?"

" It won't be easy. Not with the ship rolling like this." Madden seemed reluctant to make any admission that might detract from the immense difficulty of the job in hand.

" Of course it won't be easy. Nothing's easy. If you wanted an easy life you should never have chosen the sea."

" I'm not asking for an easy life." Madden repudiated the suggestion as though it were a slur on his character.

" So you'll get those engines going?"

" If it's possible."

" I'm relying on you," Barling said, and made it sound

like a compliment. " Just you see to things and then we'll all be happy."

Madden grunted and went away to see to things. But he looked far from happy.

Barling soon had reason to reflect that troubles never came singly. Two hours later, after the helpless ship had taken a severe battering, a particularly heavy sea burst over the port side forward of the bridge, ripped the tarpaulin off number one hatch, carried away some of the hatch-boards and poured a torrent of water into the wheat-filled hold. Mr. Thompson, the second mate, who was on watch at the time, saw what had happened and immediately reported the situation to Captain Barling.

Barling went at once to the bridge to view the damage for himself. It did not look good. The tarpaulin, still held at one end, was flapping madly in the wind like some monstrous crippled bird, while the dislodged hatch-boards were sliding about on the deck between the coaming and the bulwarks. Meanwhile, more water was continually coming over the side, foaming across the deck and adding to the hundreds of gallons that had already gone into the hold. And what made matters worse was that, lacking any engine power, it was impossible to bring the ship head-on to the sea; she just had to take it on her port beam.

" It's a nasty situation," Thompson remarked, and wished he had kept the thought unspoken, since all it earned was a scathing glance from Barling and the observation that if he could think of nothing more useful than that to say, then he had better keep quiet.

Barling sent a man to fetch Mr. Loder, but Loder had already been on his way, and it was scarcely necessary to tell him what needed doing.

" That hatch-cover will have to be replaced or we'll have number one hold flooded."

" It isn't going to be easy," Loder said; and Barling remembered that Madden had said much the same thing about fixing the engines.

" It's got to be done."

Loder nodded. " I'll go and see to it."

Rankin, the bosun, sucked his teeth loudly when he heard what was wanted and looked very doubtful.

" Christ, Mr. Loder, that's going to be a dicey job."

" Don't tell me," Loder snapped. " Round up your men. And hurry."

Rankin saw that the mate was in no mood for any argument. He hastened away to muster all available hands.

It was a small army that made its way cautiously forward under the leadership of Mr. Loder. There was a lifeline stretched between bridge and forecastle, and they had need of it, for there was no safe footing, and the press of water rolling back and forth across the heaving deck threatened to sweep their legs from under them.

They kept to the starboard side, and when they reached number one hatch Mr. Loder peered through the gap where the boards had been. The light was poor and he could see very little in the gloom; but it was not really necessary to to see anything; he knew that sea-water had gone into the hold and that it would have filtered down through the wheat. What the effect of this on the wheat would be he could only guess, but one thing was certain: it would do the wheat no good and it would do the ship no good, and the sooner the hole was plugged, the better.

He turned and yelled at Rankin: " Clear that tarpaulin. Get the boards back on."

The tarpaulin had been torn down the middle, and the two halves were flapping in the wind and making startling cracking noises, like guns firing. The bosun relayed Loder's orders, snarling savagely at the men.

" Aussie, Charlie, Ben—fetch some hammers from the fo'c'sle. You others get them boards back on." He had to shout to make himself heard above the racket of the storm.

Lawson, Wilson and Ben Grubb, a lean, middle-aged sea-man with warts on his face, clawed their way to the fore-castle, dodging past the lashing tarpaulin and battling against a sudden rush of water that came sweeping round the end of the hatch coaming. They reached the forecastle, and Lawson turned the catches and swung open the heavy steel door that gave access to the interior. He hooked the door back and they went inside, stepping over the high sill into semi-darkness. Grubb found a switch and snapped on the light. There was considerable disorder caused by the heavy rolling and pitching of the ship; neatly piled stores had been overturned and some drums of paint were career-ing from one side to the other with a noise like thunder.

" Look out," Grubb shouted, and Wilson just managed to dodge one of the drums that could easily have broken his leg.

" It's a bloody shambles," Lawson grumbled. " Why did I ever come to sea when there's all that flaming land in Australia? I must be barmy."

They found the hammers and left the forecastle for the open deck. To make conditions a shade more unpleasant, it had started to rain again; a cold, drenching downpour that made their black oilskins shine like polished metal.

Rankin saw them and shouted: " Get on with it. Knock them bloody wedges out. Look alive there " He sounded angry.

The rest of the men were still rounding up the missing hatch-boards and lifting them back into place, and Loder was helping them, not caring about rank in this emergency. Meanwhile, seas were continually breaking over the port bulwark, rushing across the deck and slopping more water into the unprotected hold. At times the men were waist-deep in the swirling torrent and in constant danger of being thrown down or smashed against winches or other rock-like objects of lethal iron. Most of them had already been down and a few had sustained minor injuries.

Lawson, Wilson and Grubb began to hammer out the wedges securing the iron batten that held the torn tarpaulin. The tarpaulin itself seemed to be doing its best to hinder the operation, lashing at them vindictively, as though with the object of driving them away. One length of it coiled itself about Wilson's body and wrenched him off his feet. He fell heavily, jarring his right shoulder, and another torrent of sea-water engulfed him, washed him free of the canvas and rolled him helplessly down to the starboard bulwalk, where he was brought to a halt by a crushing blow on the shoulders. The water ran away from him down the scuppers and he lay there for a moment, dazed, bruised and coughing up salt water, but still instinctively clinging to his hammer.

Someone stooped over him, got a hand on the collar of his coat, and hauled him up. It was the bosun.

" Come up then, can't you?" Rankin still sounded angry. He had a lot to be angry about. " What you lying down there for? Get them wedges out."

Wilson's head cleared and he went back to work. In less than half a minute the torn tarpaulin was freed and cast aside.

" Get a new tarp," Rankin shouted. " Make it lively."

They went back into the forecastle, Wilson stumbling over

the sill and falling on to a coil of rope. He could smell the strong, sweetish odour of the manila mingling with the other odours of tar and paint and oil. He heard Grubb's voice in his ear.

"You gone to sleep, boy? Or you jest giving up?"

Wilson got to his feet. The paint drums were still rolling about, but they dodged past them and found the tarpaulin folded and stowed away. It was heavy and sticky with new tar, and between them they carried it out, dodging again the rolling paint drums that threatened to cut their legs from under them.

The last of the hatch-boards had been lifted into place and there were many hands waiting to unfold the new tarpaulin. Three or four men climbed on to the hatch and took a grip on it, while Lawson, Wilson and Grubb got one end anchored with batten and wedges to the forward lip of the coaming. They began to unroll it across the boards, the men on the hatch moving backwards, bent almost double and bracing themselves to keep their balance on that erratically shifting platform. Loder, withdrawn now, his back against the starboard forecastle ladder, one hand gripping the rail, watched the operation with his hard, slate-grey eyes, missing nothing.

"Careful, boys," Rankin warned them. "Look out for yourselves now."

The warning was justified; at that moment a sea came pounding over the port side and thundered down on the deck, sweeping across the hatch. The men, caught by that sudden rush of water, felt their hands torn from the tarpaulin and themselves knocked down and rolled off the hatch and into the starboard waterway, where they lay in a tangle of arms and legs, struggling to get up.

The tarpaulin, suddenly freed, seemed to take wing as

the wind got under it. The remaining folds were unfurled in an instant, and wrenching itself from the hands of the sea-men on each side of the hatch, it rose into the air like a sail and fell against the forecastle with a tremendous crack. Loder, seeing it coming, took refuge under the ladder, but Lawson and Grubb were less fortunate; they were caught in the belly of the canvas and knocked violently down by the weight of it. The whole body of it then descended on them and held them imprisoned beneath it while they made vain efforts to grope their way out of the darkness that had so suddenly engulfed them.

Fortunately, the end batten held fast, and the rest of the men, goaded by Rankin's vituperative tongue, hastened to recapture the billowing tarpaulin and drag it back over the hatch. This time they made no mistake; exerting all their strength, they held it tight across the boards while the iron battens were slipped into the brackets and the wooden wedges beaten home.

"And now stay there, you bastard," Rankin snarled, slamming his fist on the hatch-cover. "Stay there and be damned to you!"

Rankin had got a bruised elbow and torn finger-nails, and was feeling savage. But at that he had suffered less damage than most of them. One man had a sprained wrist, and two had had teeth knocked out; all of them were going to have aches and pains and everyone was drenched to the skin. But the hatch was covered and Mr. Loder was satis-fied.

Captain Barling, watching anxiously from the bridge, was greatly relieved to see the task successfully completed; and he felt grateful to the men who had battled with the sea and the wind to accomplish it. When it came to the push they were good men, all of them; yes, very good men. He even felt an unexpected warmth towards Adam Loder, who had supervised the work. It was his duty of course; but even so. . . .

Precisely half an hour later Madden reported that the engines were ready again.

" Thank you, Chief," Barling said. " I'm obliged to you for getting the job finished so quickly."

" I thought you'd be needing the power," Madden answered dryly.

" There's nothing I need more. And again, thank you."

Soon after that the *Hopeful Enterprise* again had her head to the sea.

TEN

SEARCH

BEFORE NIGHTFALL the gale had already begun to abate its fury. Morning came with the wind fallen into a far less boisterous mood and the sea gradually following its example. There was no rain, and for the first time in days the clouds broke up to reveal large patches of blue sky.

From Barling's point of view only one thing marred the prospect, making it rather less than perfect: the *Hopeful Enterprise* was slightly down by the head and had developed a noticeable list to port. It was not difficult to divine the reason for this: the tons of sea-water that had poured into number one hold had upset the loading and had possibly caused the cargo to move despite the shifting-boards. It was not altogether out of the question that the boards had given way under the abnormal pressure, allowing the wheat to pile up on the port side. Barling considered the possibility of breaking open the hold and sending some men down with shovels to try to level out the wheat, but he decided against it. The list was not heavy enough to cause any real trouble.

He was on the bridge early, conferring with Loder in the chartroom regarding the likely position of the *India Star* after drifting in the storm.

" So you really mean to go hunting again?"

Barling lifted his gaze from the chart he was studying and turned it on the mate. " Have you any objection?"

" No. Why should I? It's just work to me."

" But you think it's a wild goose chase?"

Loder shrugged. " Shall we say that I consider the chances of success are pretty slim?"

" Very well," Barling answered coldly, " let's say that. We're going to search just the same."

There was the old cynical twist to Loder's mouth and the faint mockery in his eyes, which infuriated Barling. " In spite of the condition this ship is in?"

" There is nothing wrong with this ship. Nothing serious."

" Well, if you think so."

" I do think so."

Loder saw that nothing was going to deter Barling; he was determined to search for the *India Star*, his prize. But for how long? If they found no trace of the derelict how many days would it be before he could be persuaded to accept defeat? No telling. Barling could be a stubborn man, and there was much at stake. He might go on and on with the single-mindedness of Captain Ahab hunting for the white whale.

Loder shrugged again. " It's your decision."

The search was to be systematic. Having estimated the position to which the *India Star* might have been expected to drift, supposing that she was still afloat, the surrounding area was divided into sections, each of a width that could be surveyed from the *Hopeful Enterprise*. They would steam down the length of a section, turn and steam back along the next section, and so on until the entire area had been covered.

" It'll take time," Loder said.

" We've got time."

They began searching at first light. The day passed slowly and the sea became progressively calmer. The wind dropped to a moderate breeze and the sun shone fitfully. No ship was sighted.

The crew accepted the situation. The decision to continue the search was none of their making; they had not been consulted and would not have expected to be. But that did not prevent them from discussing the subject in the mess, and the general opinion was that Captain Barling had gone a bit wrong in the head.

Some were inclined to take a gloomy view. Ben Grubb predicted that they would just hang about until another gale hit them. "And next time it could be a hell of a lot worse. We've shipped a deal of water in that for'ard hold as it is, and there's a list."

" Not much of a list," Lawson said.

" It could get worse. The wheat must've shifted and it's soaked with water. Maybe that'll make it swell, set up pressure. No telling what may happen."

Lawson gave a laugh. " I don't know why you're so keen to get home, chum. If I had an eye like yours I'd want it got right before I stepped ashore."

Grubb had come out of the argument with the tarpaulin sporting a black eye and a split lip. It could have been that which was making him moody.

" Just say I want to get home," he said. " And if it's left to the Old Man I ain't so sure I will—ever."

" You can't do much else 'cept leave it to him," Veevers said. " He's the gaffer and it's his say so."

" So much the worse for us."

" Could be the better for us."

" How d'you make that out?"

Veevers looked knowing. " When there's salvage money

going around everybody gets a share, don't they?"

They all stared at him. " Is that so? You mean we all get something?"

" That's the way I heard it. If we get that ship we'll all be richer."

It put a different complexion on the matter.

" Well, in that case," Lawson said, " I'm with the Old Man, looney or not."

There was considerable agreement on that point now that the financial aspect had been explained by Veevers, and only Grubb struck a discordant note. " Gah!" he said. " We won't never find that ship, so what's the odds?"

Trubshaw was another one who was not feeling happy. In fact, he was feeling about as bad as a man could feel. The gale had shaken him up a good deal, especially during that period when the engines had been out of action and the ship had been rolling helplessly in the grip of the sea. Trubshaw had done his best to wedge himself in the bunk in such a way as to avoid being tossed about, but had not been successful, and his injured neck had given him so much pain that he had cried out in agony. The pain was there all the time, but when the bunk almost stood on end, throwing him this way and that, it stabbed him like a sharp knife. There was in addition a throbbing ache in his head and a general feeling of sickness, both physical and mental.

Orwell visited him again and did nothing to cheer him up. Trubshaw told Orwell about his sickness because he felt that he had to confide in someone; but Orwell just laughed.

" You're seasick, Trub. I thought you'd be hardened to it after all the years you've put in."

Trubshaw scowled at him. " Seasick, my arse! I ain't never been seasick in my life."

" There's always a first time."

" I tell you it ain't seasickness. I'm ill."

Orwell looked at him without sympathy. " You're ill sure enough. Much pain in that neck?"

" Pain! It's bloody agony."

" I'm not surprised. You thought about what I said?"

" Abaht what you said?" There was panic in Trubshaw's eyes and Orwell was delighted to see it.

" About dying."

" I ain't goin' to die."

" I hope not, Trub, for your sake. But every day we spend looking for that other ship makes it more likely. Got to face facts, haven't we, Trub?"

Trubshaw said bitterly: " The Old Man's crazy. Don't 'e know I need 'ospital treatment?"

Orwell looked down at him, smiling faintly. " Just atween you and me, Trub, I doubt if the Old Man ever gave you a thought when he decided to go after the *India Star*. He's got other things on his mind."

Some time after Orwell had gone away, leaving Trubshaw even more depressed than he had been before the visit, the second steward, a slim young man named Tricker, came in to see whether the invalid wanted anything.

" I wanter see the Old Man," Trubshaw said.

Tricker pulled doubtfully at his lower lip. He had a pasty complexion with a tendency to acne and a lot of fair hair that completely covered his ears and flopped over the collar of his blue steward's jacket.

" Now why would you be wanting to see him?"

" Never you mind," Trubshaw said. " 'Tain't none o' your business. You jus' get 'im 'ere."

" And suppose Captain Barling don't want to see you?"

" You can suppose wotcher bleedin' like, mate. Cos 'e's got to, ain't he? It's my right, innit?"

" I don't know about that," Tricker said. " I don't know nothing about rights."

Trubshaw thrust out a hand and gripped the sleeve of Tricker's jacket, and the pain that this movement caused him gave a hard edge to his voice. " You get 'im, see? You get 'im down 'ere, an' look sharp abaht it."

Tricker was overawed. He knew Trubshaw's reputation and he had no wish to get on the wrong side of him.

" All right then. I'll see what I can do."

Trubshaw released his arm. " You do that. An' you make sure 'e comes. Not termorrer neither, nor the nex' day. Now. You get me?"

The second steward carried Trubshaw's message to Barling, who was in his cabin making some calculations on a sheet of paper. Glancing at them, Tricker noted that they involved sums of money; rather large sums. Barling turned the sheet over, hiding the figures.

" Why does he wish to see me?"

" He didn't say, sir. But he was very insistent. He said it was his right."

" Very well. I'll see him."

" Yes, sir." Tricker felt relieved. He would not have relished going back and informing Trubshaw that his request had been refused. " I'll go and tell him."

Barling waited until Tricker had left the cabin, then picked up the sheet of paper on which he had been making his calculations. He stared at the figures for a few moments, and then with an exclamation of impatience he crumpled the sheet into a ball and stuffed it in his pocket. Where was the point in making calculations when there were so many uncertainties, chief of which was the finding of a drifting, derelict ship which might already be at the bottom of the ocean?

He wondered what Trubshaw wished to see him about. He had already paid a couple of visits to the injured man and could not imagine why he should have sent this urgent message for another. But there was one certain way of finding the answer.

Tricker was still with Trubshaw when Barling walked in, but he left at once. Barling looked at Trubshaw, and it needed no great powers of perception to divine that the seaman was worried. He looked ill too, but that was only natural in the circumstances.

"Well, Trubshaw," Barling said. "What's troubling you?"

"I feel bad, sir."

Barling nodded. "I'd be surprised if you didn't. Can't expect to get over a thing like this in a couple of days, you know."

"I'm a sick man, sir. Real sick."

"You'll feel better in a day or two."

"I ain't countin' on it." Trubshaw sounded very gloomy, and looked it. "I could be worse."

"No reason why you should be."

"I need proper treatment."

"You're getting the best we can provide. In the absence of a qualified doctor—"

"That's just it," Trubshaw cut in. "In the absence of a qualified doctor I could easily die."

"Oh, nonsense! No need to talk about dying. You're not as bad as that."

"You don't know 'ow bad I am. Nobody don't. I oughter

be in 'ospital. I oughter 'ave this 'ere neck X-razed. It could turn to gangrene."

"Gangrene! What on earth makes you think that?" Barling looked at Trubshaw closely. "Has someone been putting ideas into your head?"

"Nobody's been puttin' ideas into my 'ead," Trubshaw said sullenly. "I can think things aht for myself. An' what I says is this: I oughter be gettin' proper medical attention, not this Boy Scout stuff."

"You'll get all the attention you need as soon as we reach port."

"Ah, but when'll that be?" Trubshaw's eyes stared accusingly at Barling. "The way I 'eard it, we ain't even makin' for port yet. Is that right, sir?"

Barling had to admit that it was.

"I don't think it's right." There was a whining note in Trubshaw's voice. "Wiv a sick man on board you oughter be 'eadin' straight for 'ome, not 'angin' arahnd 'ere lookin' for that there ship. If you ask my opinion, she ain't afloat any more anyway."

"I am not asking your opinion, Trubshaw." Barling's voice was icy.

"Well, are you goin' to get me 'ome to a real 'ospital?"

"All in good time."

"Which means you won't call off this flamin' search?"

"I see no reason to."

"No reason to! Ain't my life reason enough?"

"Your life isn't in the balance, Trubshaw. You aren't nearly as bad as you seem to think. I certainly cannot alter my plans to suit you."

Barling walked towards the door. Trubshaw stared at him with hatred. "Damn you then! Damn you for a 'eartless bastard!" He felt like weeping. Barling didn't care; he was perfectly willing to let a man die rather than interfere with plans already made. "You won't get away with this. I'll make complaints. I'll complain to the Seamen's Union. They'll bring charges an' you'll be up in court. You can't jus' let me die."

"If you die," Barling said coolly, "it might be rather difficult for you to complain to the Union. My advice to you is to forget about it and go to sleep." He went out and closed the door behind him.

Trubshaw lay in the bunk trembling with rage and frustration and fear. The more he thought about it, the more he became convinced that Barling expected him to die. That was why he was refusing to alter his plans. He had no intention of giving up the search and heading for port because he was sure it would be a waste of time. And it was no use threatening him with Union action because, as he himself had pointed out, a dead man could make no complaint.

"I'm goin' to die," Trubshaw muttered. "Oh, Gawd! I'm goin' to die. Nobody cares."

In fact, he was not altogether correct in thinking that. Barling did care. He was more than a little worried about Trubshaw; and though he still thought Trubshaw was exaggerating the seriousness of his condition, there might be something in what the man had said. It was a very nasty wound he had in his neck and there could be no doubt that it ought to have professional attention. Therefore, it was not without some misgiving that Barling decided nevertheless to go on with the search and ignore Trubshaw's plea. He tried to convince himself that Trubshaw's life was in no danger, but in spite of everything there persisted in the back of his mind a small grain of doubt, of disquiet, even of guilt. For he knew that if he had not insisted on taking the *India Star* in tow in the first place Trubshaw would never have sustained his injury; and he knew also that, but for this continued search, they could have reached port and packed the man off to hospital within three or four days; whereas, even if they sighted the *India Star* before nightfall, it would take a lot longer than that because of the slowness of the tow. Yet he had to do it; he could not give up now. For Ann's sake he had to go through with it.

Barling questioned Scotton regarding the *Atlantic Scavenger*. He was still afraid that the tug might steal his prize.

" What's the latest from them?"

" Nothing," Scotton said. " The last signal I picked up was yesterday. Since then I haven't heard anything."

" Perhaps they gave up."

" It seems likely, sir. I think they'd come to the conclusion that it was a pretty useless quest."

" Well, let me know if you hear anything," Barling said.

Scotton took this for a dismissal and went away.

The search continued until the gathering darkness made it useless to go on any longer; then Barling called it off until morning. During the night the wind dropped away almost completely, and dawn came with a thin fog reducing visibility.

" This isn't going to help the search," Loder remarked when Barling joined him on the bridge towards the end of the morning watch. " All we needed was fog."

" It's nothing much," Barling said. " It'll clear when the sun comes up."

" Perhaps." Loder was his usual disgruntled self at that hour, unwilling to look on the bright side of anything; unwilling even to admit that there was a bright side.

Barling ignored him; he did not require Loder's gloomy remarks to depress him; the fog was enough to do that, even though it was thin, even though it might disperse later. It was not enough to prevent them from re-starting the search, but it limited the width of the sections and made the operation that much slower. Still, there was nothing one could do to control the weather; its vagaries had to be accepted. One thing at least was certain: with little or no wind, the *India Star* would not be drifting so much. If she was drifting at all.

By ten o'clock a hazy sun was visible through the mist, which was becoming patchy. And then, at precisely eleven-fifteen, they found what they were looking for. When probably no one in the entire ship except the captain still had any belief that it could happen, they sighted the *India Star*.

"There!" Mr. Walpole shouted, pointing excitedly. "There, sir! Can you see her?"

She appeared out of the mist like a wraith, her outline blurred and indistinct. Barling looked at the ship, half fearful that it might dissolve and fade into nothing even as he watched. So he was vindicated; he had been right, the others wrong. The prize was here.

Breaking in upon his thoughts came the third mate's voice: "I didn't think we'd find her. I felt sure she would have sunk."

Yes, they had all thought that, and they had all been wrong. Only he had been right. But he did not feel any great pride in that; he had not persisted merely to prove who was right and who was wrong; that was of no importance. What was important was that they should take this ship again in tow and bring her safely to port. He was only too well aware that there was still a long way to go before that goal could be reached.

He gave an order and Walpole relayed it to the helmsman. The *Hopeful Enterprise* altered course slightly and headed towards the derelict. A few minutes later Walpole, who had been examining the gradually hardening lines of the *India Star* through his binoculars, gave an exclamation of surprise.

" That's funny, sir."

" What is," Barling asked.

" There's no smoke."

It was true. With the mist thinning around the *India Star* it was possible to see that there was no column of smoke rising from the midships section.

" The fire must have gone out, sir."

Either it had burnt itself out or the torrential rain had quenched it. At last things seemed to be in Barling's favour. The gods were smiling.

Half an hour later the *Hopeful Enterprise* was hove to and number one lifeboat was being swung out under the direction of Mr. Loder. He had decided to take the same boarding party as before—Orwell, Lawson, Veevers and Wilson—and again he felt that spark of enthusiasm leaping up inside him. It had died when they had lost touch with the *India Star*; he had never expected to see the ship again, and he had thought Barling a fool for going on with the search; but now they had found the prize once more, and once more the idea of taking it in against all the odds roused his spirit.

And this time the fixing of the tow-rope ought not to be so difficult; the sea was calmer and there was scarcely any wind. The *Hopeful Enterprise* had been able to get in closer, and that meant that there would be less weight of hawser to haul across. Yes, indeed the gods were smiling.

And then they ceased to smile. Or perhaps the smile had turned a trifle cynical.

" Sir!" Mr. Walpole said; and there was something in his tone that caused Barling to swing round quickly.

The third mate was pointing again. Barling followed the direction of his outstretched arm and saw what it was that had caught his attention. It was away on the starboard bow, and he did not need to use his binoculars; he knew only too well what that shape was just emerging from the thinning mist, and he knew why Walpole had said " Sir!" in that particular tone of voice. It was a small, squat, unmistakable vessel, and it was the vessel he least desired to see in that precise place at that precise moment of time.

" The tug," Walpole said.

The *Atlantic Scavenger* had not after all abandoned the search.

ELEVEN

VOLUNTEER

MR. LODER swore briefly. So it had become a race. But it was a race that they must surely win, for the tug was at least a mile away.

"They're too late," Orwell said. "They'll never catch us now."

Loder snapped an order: "Man the boat."

The tug would come up fast when her master had sized up the situation. There was no time to lose.

On the bridge Barling and Walpole caught the flicker of an Aldis lamp sending its message across the intervening stretch of water. They both read it.

"Leave her to us."

Barling spoke calmly to Walpole, and the third mate picked up an Aldis lamp and sent back an answer.

"We were here first."

More flashes from the tug. "We are going to tow her in."

An answer from the *Hopeful Enterprise*: "No. We are."

From the tug: "Do not interfere."

And finally from the *Hopeful Enterprise*: "Go to hell."

"Lower away," Loder ordered.

The lifeboat dropped a little jerkily towards the water as the falls were paid out, and a few moments later it was moving away from the side of the ship, its engine pulsing and exhaust fumes puffing from the stern. The *Atlantic Scavenger* was still more than half a mile away from the boat, but they could see her bluff bows and the compact bridge and funnel.

" She might as well give up," Lawson said. " We've got her beat."

It certainly looked like it. The boat had only a hundred yards to go and would reach the *India Star* in less than a minute. But Lawson had spoken too soon; perhaps tempting fate. Indeed, he had scarcely finished speaking when the engine of the lifeboat stammered a little, seemed to choke once or twice, and then fell silent. The boat began to drift.

They tried to re-start the engine, but without success; it remained obstinately unresponsive to all their efforts, and the tug halved the distance between them. They could hear the rushing sound of its bow wave coming rapidly nearer.

" Man the oars," Loder snarled. " Look lively."

They had to depend on their own strength now. They slipped the crutches into their sockets and took up the heavy oars. They took up positions on the thwarts and rested the oars in the crutches.

" Together, pull!"

They began to row. The boat moved sluggishly forward and the *India Star* seemed to be farther away. Loder, still with his hand on the tiller, glanced over his shoulder and saw that the tug was near.

" Put your backs into it."

The men pulled with a will. It was a personal affair with them all now. The tug was the enemy and they meant to beat it; they and Loder were in full agreement on that point.

But there were still fifty yards of open water separating them from the *India Star* when the tug overhauled them. It came in at an angle, slanting across the line on which they were moving, and it seemed scarcely to slacken speed at all.

"By God!" Veevers shouted in sudden alarm. "They're going to run us down."

Loder saw the danger at the same instant. It seemed incredible that the tugmaster should take such drastic action, but he could see a valuable prize slipping through his fingers, and that was enough to make any man desperate.

"Back together!"

They backed water, pushing on the looms of the oars, and the tug swept past within a few feet of the boat's bows. Loder could see faces peering down from the bridge of the little ship; hard, grim faces under peaked caps. He felt like shouting at them, cursing their inhumanity; but it would have been pointless. And then the bow wave hit the boat, and it was tossing about and twisting round, with water spilling over the gunwale; and for a few moments there was utter confusion as the men strove to hold on to their oars and regain control.

It was possible that the tugmaster had intended doing no more than this, hoping that the subsequent confusion in the lifeboat might give him time to get his own boarding party on to the deck of the *India Star*. But the very speed of his approach militated against the success of the manoeuvre, for he could neither draw alongside the derelict nor launch his own boat until way had been taken off the tug. And by then Loder and his crew had regained control of the lifeboat and were well on the way to closing the last few yards of water between them and the Jacob's-ladder still hanging down from the bulwarks of the *India Star*.

They took in their oars and the boat nudged the side of the ship. Lawson grabbed the Jacob's-ladder, and Loder swarmed nimbly up and jumped down on to the deck. He turned and saw the tug some distance away, hove to, a boat being launched. He grinned sardonically. They were too late. He was in possession now and, do what they would, they could not shift him.

Orwell came up over the bulwark and made fast the painter. The other men followed. They could hear the muffled beat of the engine in the boat that was now drawing away from the *Atlantic Scavenger*.

" We're going to have visitors," Veevers remarked.

" No one," Loder said, " is to be allowed to set foot on this deck. Is that understood?"

Lawson nodded. " Understood, sir." He began to climb back over the bulwark.

" Where are you going?" Loder demanded.

" Won't be a moment, sir."

Watched by the others, Lawson went quickly down the Jacob's-ladder, picked up a boat-hook from the lifeboat and returned with it in his hand.

" Prepared to repel boarders, sir."

Veevers gave him a pat on the back. " Good for you Aussie."

" I think we could have persuaded them without that,' Loder said.

Lawson grinned. " It'll strengthen the argument. If they try any tricks I don't mind giving 'em a jab with the sharp end of this. They gave us a nasty minute or two out there and I haven't forgotten it. Things like that stick in my gullet."

They stood by the bulwark and watched the other boat. They waited in silence as it eased alongside the lifeboat. There were four men in it. One of them stepped over the gunwale and across a thwart of the lifeboat and began to climb the Jacob's-ladder. He was a chunky man and the life-jacket he was wearing made him look even chunkier. His face looked like a slab of raw beef with a couple of indentations in it to accommodate his eyes, a blob for a nose and a slit for a mouth. The whole thing might have been dashed off by an amateur sculptor on a bad day.

Loder allowed him to get half-way up the ladder and then said: "You can stop there."

The man stopped. He said: "I'm the mate of the *Atlantic Scavenger*. Name's Creegan."

"My name's Loder, and I'm mate of the *Hopeful Enterprise*. What do you want?"

"I'd like to come on board, Mr. Loder."

"Sorry, Mr. Creegan; that won't be possible."

"To hell with that," Creegan said, and he started climbing again.

Lawson leaned over the bulwark and prodded him with the boat-hook. Creegan stopped.

"So that's the way it is."

"That's the way it is," Loder said.

"You know we've come out to bring this ship in?"

"That won't be necessary. We're bringing her in."

Creegan glanced back at the *Hopeful Enterprise* and then up again at Loder. There was an expression of disbelief on his beefy face. "You'd never make it."

"Think not?"

"I'm bloody sure not."

"If you stick around," Loder said, "you can watch us try."

Creegan hung on to the Jacob's-ladder and appeared uncertain what to do next. It was obvious that he was reluctant to go back to the tug and report failure; yet, with Lawson holding the boat-hook ready, there was no hope of forcing his way on board the *India Star*.

" You can't be serious about this."

" I'm not joking."

" But you'd never be able to tow her in."

" What makes you think not?" Loder asked. " We towed her for nearly two days before the hawser parted in the storm."

Creegan's eyes narrowed. " So that's how she got here. That explains it."

" You've been wondering about that?"

" You bet we've been wondering about it." Creegan sounded exasperated. " You've given us some trouble finding this baby."

" Well, now you've found her you can shove off," Loder said. " We've got work to do."

" You really mean to go ahead with this, don't you?"

" We do. You can go back and tell your skipper that."

Creegan hesitated. As if to help him make up his mind, Lawson reached over the bulwark and prodded him again with the boat-hook, none too gently. Creegan took the hint and went back to his boat. They heard him snarl an order, and the boat moved away and headed for the *Atlantic Scavenger*. The four seamen on the deck of the *India Star* gave a mocking cheer to speed it on its way and added a few rude gestures for good measure.

" That's enough," Loder said sharply. " We've no time to waste on courtesies. Get moving."

The broken hawser was still hanging from the fairlead in the bows, more than a hundred fathoms of it stretching down into the water beneath the ship. They had to jettison it before starting to haul the new one across, and throughout the whole operation the tug stood by, keeping an eye on things but making no move to interfere.

"Why don't they piss off?" Veevers said. "There ain't nothing for them here. Not now."

"There could be," Orwell said.

"How d'you mean?"

Orwell pulled thoughtfully at his beard. "Suppose the tow was to part again. If they was still hanging around they could nip in and snap up the jackpot. My bet is they'll tail us."

Loder had already come to the same conclusion and he was not altogether happy about it. "What we really need is a salvage crew to stay on board. Nobody could take her then. Just a couple of men would be enough."

Veevers looked doubtfully towards the bridge. There was admittedly no smoke rising now, but that was not to say that the fire would not break out again or that there would not be another explosion. And there was that list too; a little worse than it had been before.

"You ain't asking any of us to stay on board, are you, sir?"

"No," Loder said. "It was just a thought. But of course it would not be reasonable to ask anyone to do that. Too risky."

And then Wilson said quietly: "I don't mind staying."

Four pairs of eyes turned in his direction, and under that combined stare he looked slightly embarrassed.

"You?" Loder said.

And Veevers said: "You're barmy. You won't get me to keep you company."

"I don't want anyone to keep me company." Wilson looked at Loder. "I suppose one man would be enough, sir? It's just a legal point, isn't it?"

Loder rasped his chin. "I suppose so. But it's out of the question. I couldn't leave you behind."

" But I want to stay." There was a strange eagerness in Wilson's voice that puzzled Loder. The young seaman actually seemed to be afraid that he would not be allowed to remain on board the *India Star*.

" You want to?"

" Yes, sir."

" Why?"

" I don't know. It's just something. This whole ship to myself. I'd like it."

" Barmy," Veevers muttered. " Proper barmy."

Loder was silent, thinking it over. It was a risk; but, after all, the *India Star* had proved herself seaworthy by coming through one storm, so there was no reason why she should sink now. And there was that tug standing by like a damned vulture. Loder hated the thought of losing the prize now, and if Wilson was prepared, even eager, to provide a little extra insurance, why stop him?

" Very well," he said, " if that's what you really want to do. You won't be short of food; there's bound to be plenty of that on board."

" And you can sleep in the captain's cabin," Lawson said. " You'll be moving up in the world."

" All right," Loder said. " That's enough. Back to the boat."

Orwell, Lawson and Veevers climbed over the bulwark and went down the Jacob's-ladder. Wilson could hear the wooden rungs tapping against the side of the ship as they descended. Loder turned for a final word.

" If you're in trouble you can always signal us."

" I'm not a signaller, sir."

" Well, just stand on the fo'c'sle and wave some flags, any flags. If it's dark you can flash a light." He did not add that if Wilson was in trouble it would probably be impossible for anyone on board the *Hopeful Enterprise* to do anything about it. There was no point in discouraging the volunteer.

He walked to the bulwark and climbed over. He gave a last nod to Wilson. " Good luck, then."

" Thank you, sir," Wilson said.

He watched them rowing back to the *Hopeful Enterprise*, and he had an impulse to call them back, to say he had changed his mind; but he did not do so. The deck moved under his feet and a pulley-block rattled. There was no other sound. He turned away from the bulwark and looked towards the bridge. No one there; deserted; dead. He shivered, sensing for the first time the eeriness of this silent ship. He remembered that men had died in her; their bodies would still be there unless the fire had burnt them. Perhaps their ghosts would haunt the *India Star*, lurking in the cabins and gliding along the alleyways where in life the men had moved.

But that was nonsense. He had better keep that kind of stuff out of his head. There were no such things as ghosts, and if there were, it would not be dead seamen who would come to haunt him; it would be the woman he had left dead in Montreal. And she did haunt him—in the mind. Waking or sleeping, she was there, never to be shaken off.

He took a grip on himself. There was no point in just standing there; he had to be doing something. And the first thing to do was to make a survey of what was to be his home for several days at least.

It was the wreckage amidships that drew him first, as it had drawn Loder on a previous occasion. He saw the toppled funnel, and, like Loder, he crawled to the edge of the wide, jagged hole in the decks and peered down. There was no smoke now to obscure the view, and he could see right down to the engine-room which the explosion had wrecked and the fire had gutted. He caught a glint of something down there, of something moving, and he heard the sound of water swilling back and forth as the ship rolled. There was the reason why the fire had gone out; the engine-room was flooded. He wondered whether this water had all got in from above or whether some of it was leaking in from the bottom; but either way there was nothing he could do about it unless he got a bucket and line and started baling.

Then he saw the impaled head, and it was as much a shock as if he had in fact seen a ghost. It was the unexpectedness of it that touched his nerves; for Loder had said nothing to anyone about what he had seen. It was completely black now, and but for the lank, straight hair, might have been the head of a Negro. Wilson stared at it for a while in fascination, then drew back with a shudder.

As he did so he felt what seemed like an answering shudder pass through the ship. He got to his feet, ran to the bridge and looked towards the bows. The hawser stretched away from the forecastle in a gentle curve before dipping beneath the surface of the water, and two or three hundred yards ahead was the stern of the *Hopeful Enterprise*. Smoke was pouring from her funnel, and a breeze that had sprung up and had already dispersed the last of the fog was blowing this smoke away in a widening, thinning streamer.

They were on their way.

Wilson looked for the *Atlantic Scavenger* and found her some distance away on the port beam. He lifted two fingers to the tug and went below.

Everywhere he went he saw the unmistakable signs of a hasty evacuation. There were bunks that had been slept in and left as they were, the sheets and blankets all in disarray; in the crew's messroom aft there were plates and cups left unwashed, and dishes that had had food on them were spilled over on to the deck. It looked as though the decision to abandon the ship, when it had finally been taken, had been taken suddenly. Possibly there had been some urging from the master of the *Sargasso Queen*, and with a fire burning amidships and the weather breaking up, Captain van Donck of the *India Star* had no doubt decided that he had no alternative. And so the prize had been left for anyone who could take it.

Again, as he explored the ship, Wilson had that sense of eeriness. To him, a seaman, everything was familiar; he could find his way with ease; but it was the absence of any other human being that was so unnerving. He found himself continually glancing over his shoulder, expecting to discover eyes watching his every movement; or, opening a door, he would imagine that someone had just slipped away, avoiding him. And there was the silence: no thump of engines, no sound of voices; only the whisper of the sea moving along the sides and the occasional clatter of something loose moving as the ship rolled and setting the pulse racing.

As Lawson had suggested, he moved into the captain's quarters; there was no reason why he should not take the best. There was plenty of room, very different from the cramped accommodation he shared in the *Hopeful Enterprise*. There was a day cabin comfortably furnished with armchairs and a settee, a desk, bookshelves, even a carpet; all this abandoned to the sea. The inner cabin was smaller. Wilson looked into the wardrobe. Captain van Donck had left his tropical kit and a spare blue serge jacket with brass buttons and four gold braid rings on each sleeve. Wilson took the jacket out and tried it on; it was loose round the waist, obviously made for a much stouter man. He took the jacket off and put it back in the wardrobe.

Another door opened into a small bathroom, gleaming with chromium plate, glass and white porcelain. Wilson caught sight of his reflection in a mirror; the face looked older, the eyes troubled; it had the traces too of the beating he had received from Trubshaw, but he was not worried about that; if that had been all there was on his mind he would have been happy. If only it were possible to turn back the calendar, to start again from that fatal moment when he had gone ashore with Trubshaw and Lawson and Moir. If only he had been able then to foresee what would happen. But it was too late to think of that now. He was caught; he was in a net from which there was no escape. The haunted eyes stared back at him from the mirror and could see no way out. Except one.

He left the bathroom and went back into the day cabin. He walked to the desk and started opening drawers. There was nothing of much interest to him; it was hardly likely that there would be. Captain van Donck would have seen to it that all papers of any importance were taken with him when he left the ship.

One drawer was locked. Wilson searched for a key but without success. He shrugged; it did not matter. He moved away from the desk, but illogically the locked drawer drew him back. Why had it been left locked when none of the others were? Had it simply been overlooked or had it purposely been left like that? Yet why would anyone bother to lock a drawer in a ship that was going to sink anyway? But of course there had been no certainty that the ship would sink. And it had not done so.

The question nagged at Wilson; key or no key, he had to open the drawer and see for himself what was inside.

It was was surprisingly easy to force the drawer; he had only to insert the blade of his knife and exert a little pressure. Inside were a .38 calibre revolver and several boxes of ammunition.

TWELVE

GUN PLAY

BARLING WAS not altogether happy when Loder returned from the *India Star* without Wilson. It seemed to him a grave risk to leave the young seaman on board the other ship.

" He wanted to stay," Loder explained.

To Barling that appeared hardly sufficient reason. Perhaps Wilson did not fully realise the danger, but Loder should have done so, and should not have allowed him to stay.

" I don't like it."

" You want that ship, don't you?"

" Of course I want the ship, but that's not the point."

" I think it's very much the point," Loder said. " The tug is going to shadow us; you can count on that. And if the *India Star* goes adrift again they'll maybe get in quicker than we can. Wilson is our insurance against a take-over."

Barling could see that without its being spelt out to him. Indeed, with a part of his mind he was glad that Wilson had been left behind to guard the prize, though he would not admit as much to Loder.

" It's risking a man's life."

Loder's mouth had its sardonic twist as he asked: " Do you want us to go back and take him off?"

Presented with a straight question like that, Barling was forced to make his own decision; obviously Loder was not going to let him shift the responsibility. He hesitated a moment before answering: " No. Since he's there, we'll leave it like that for the present. But get one of the engineers to look at the engine in that boat."

" I was going to do that."

" I may decide to take Wilson off—later."

" Yes," Loder said. " Later." But his eyes seemed to be saying that it would be much later, that he did not believe Barling would decide on anything of the kind. Wilson was the insurance, and it was too valuable a piece of insurance to throw away.

Trubshaw, lying on his bunk in the hospital with his head aching and his neck hurting him, listened to the sounds of the ship and tried to deduce from them what was going on. When the engines stopped he wondered whether they had broken down again; but then he heard the sounds of the boat being lowered and he guessed that the *India Star* had been sighted. It was not until the second steward came in that he heard about the *Atlantic Scavenger*.

" You mean the tug's 'ere?"

" That's right," Tricker said. " It was touch and go whether she got in first, but we beat her to it." He sounded complacent, as though he personally had won the race.

" You mean we ain't goin' to let 'er 'ave the tow?"

" After all the trouble we've taken to get it? You must be joking."

Trubshaw groaned. " We should've let it go. We should've let the tug take it. It's 'ers be rights."

" Not the way I heard it," Tricker said. " You take a ship what's been abandoned, it's anybody's to take in tow what can. And it's first come, first served."

" We oughter let it go."

" What and lose all that salvage money? There's a whisper going round that we'll all get some. Nice work, I call that."

Trubshaw felt the vibration as the engines started to turn over and knew that the *Hopeful Enterprise* must be taking up the slack. He groaned again.

" I'll never get no money. I'll be dead."

Tricker looked at him with a sharp, calculating eye and came to the conclusion that Trubshaw could just possibly be right; he certainly did not look at all well. Not that he, Tricker, was going to lose any sleep over it. It was someone else's worry: Trubshaw's.

Wilson took the revolver out of the drawer and examined it. There was a thin film of oil on the surface of the metal to protect it from rust, and the barrel was about six inches long. On the side of the barrel he could read the words: Smith & Wesson. He had never before had a real pistol in his hands, and he felt a thrill at the touch of it, at the dull gleam of the dark metal. It looked as deadly as a cobra; two and a half pounds of compact lethal machinery. Wilson gripped the butt in the palm of his hand, curled one finger round the trigger and eased back the hammer with his thumb. He held the revolver at arm's length and pressed the trigger. The hammer tripped forward with a sharp click.

" Bang!" Wilson said. " You're dead."

After a little manipulation he found how to get at the cylinder for loading. He took six rounds from one of the boxes and filled the cylinder. He felt a desire to fire the gun; he was like a child with a new toy and could not wait to use it. Well, what was there to stop him? On board this ship he was master; he could do what he liked and there was no one to tell him not to. So he would fire the revolver.

He put a box of ammunition in his pocket, and with the

revolver in his hand, left the cabin. He did not want to risk attracting attention from the *Hopeful Enterprise*, so he made his way to the poop and took up a position on the starboard side of the deckhouse where he was also screened from the view of anyone on board the tug. The stern of the *India Star* was lifting and falling, so that he had to steady himself with his left hand on a stanchion while he lifted the revolver, sighted on a fleck of foam on the surface of a wave and pressed the trigger.

He was surprised by the kick of recoil; it jarred his hand. The barrel jumped and he had no idea where the bullet went. He realised that accurate shooting with a pistol was not quite as easy as it looked on the films.

He tried again, gripping the butt more firmly and keeping his arm as rigid as possible. This time he did in fact see where the bullet hit the water, though it was not quite where he had aimed. The third and fourth shots he lost altogether, but the fifth he again saw flick the water. The sixth was nowhere.

That completed one loading. He ejected the empty cases and refilled the cylinder. The crack of the revolver sounded quite loud in his ears, but he doubted whether it would be noticed in the other ships; the wind would carry it away. He continued firing until he had used up the box of ammunition; then he returned to the cabin, cleaned and oiled the gun, and put it back in the drawer.

He had had nothing to eat since breakfast, and he suddenly realised that he was hungry. He searched around and found a steward's pantry stocked with food. There was a sink and a small cooker with a cylinder of gas connected to it. He cooked himself a meal and drank three cups of sweet, milky coffee.

When he went back to the bridge he saw that the sky

had cleared and that a pale sun was throwing shadows on the deck. The shadows moved as the ship rolled, and the wind seemed to have turned colder, though it had not increased in strength. There was a slight swell, but nothing to worry about; if it got no worse than this, Wilson reflected, they would make it easily. And then what? The police waiting for him? His heart sank. What future was there for him?

Scotton came to Barling with information early the next day. He seemed excited about it.

" The cat's out of the bag, sir."

Barling, who with so many things on his mind had not slept well, looked at him sourly. " What do you mean? What cat?"

" The news, sir."

" What news? For God's sake, man, out with it."

" About us, sir. About us snatching the *India Star* from the tug. They must have sent a signal from the *Atlantic Scavenger* about it."

" Yes, they would. It was to be expected." Barling thought it over. It made no difference of course; the situation remained the same; it had simply become common knowledge, as it had been bound to sooner or later. " Well, much good it'll do them."

" I suppose, sir, there's no need to maintain radio silence any longer?"

" What? Oh, no, not any more." There had been no point in it from the moment when the tug had sighted them, but he had forgotten to tell Scotton; there had been so many other matters to think about. " Back to normal."

" Yes, sir." Scotton sounded pleased. Now that the ban had been lifted he would be able to give the other side of

the story. There would be people in England eager to hear
something from the *Hopeful Enterprise*, and he would satisfy
them. He might even get his name in the papers. It looked
like being a big story.

Barling, as though able to read what was passing in
Scotton's mind, applied a little cold water to the flames of
the radio officer's enthusiasm. "Nothing sensational, you
understand? No playing this up as some kind of piracy on
the high seas. Just the bare facts and no embroidery."

Scotton went away slightly deflated but consoling himself
with the reflection that even the bare facts were pretty sensational. They hardly needed any embroidery.

The second day on board the *India Star* passed rather
slowly for Wilson. He felt restless. Like Captain Barling, he
had not slept well, and for a similar reason: there was too
much on his mind; though what was on Wilson's mind was
very different from what was on Barling's. At first light he
was up on the forecastle examining the hawser where it
passed through the fairlead. There were no obvious signs
of wear or strain. He had thoroughly greased the wire the
previous day and it was making very little noise.

He went back to the bridge and searched for the tug with
the aid of a powerful pair of binoculars that he had found in
the wheelhouse. He discovered the *Atlantic Scavenger* away
on the horizon on the port side. The night had passed and
nothing had changed. The weather was dry, the wind fresh,
just enough sea running to make the ship roll, visibility good.

Wilson was observed from the *Hopeful Enterprise* when
he came out on to the wing of the bridge or went up to the
forecastle. Barling himself had a look at him through binoculars and was somewhat relieved. His qualms of the
previous day concerning the young seaman's safety appeared

now to have had little foundation. Wilson was obviously all right; probably enjoying the experience. It would be an adventure to him, something to talk about when he went ashore.

But Wilson was not looking upon it as an adventure that he would talk about ashore. Drawn irresistibly by that gruesome blackened head impaled on its iron spike, he returned to the boat-deck and peered down into the hole. He heard the dark water swilling back and forth at the bottom and imagined that he heard the cries of the dead men. He looked at the head and wondered what kind of man this had been in life. One of the joking kind perhaps. He was not joking now, unless this was in itself a joke, this head caught up on the iron and staring blindly at nothing.

He saw the rats then, a dozen of them, creeping along some broken decking, only dimly discernible in the half-light. He could hear them squeaking, and they disgusted him, turned his stomach. He hated rats.

On a sudden impulse he stood up and ran to the captain's cabin and fetched the revolver. He lay down at the edge of the hole and saw that one of the rats had succeeded in climbing up to the head. It was gnawing away at that grim relic, and Wilson could hear the sound of its teeth grinding into flesh and bone. He steadied the revolver with both hands, took careful aim, and fired.

The sound of the shot was followed by an immediate scamper of small feet as the rats fled to safety. The bullet had missed the rat that had been gnawing the head but had struck the head itself, wrenching it from the spike and sending it plummeting to the bottom of the ship. Wilson heard the splash as it hit the water; it was like the sound of a large stone dropped into a well.

He was angered by his failure to kill the rat. " Damn

you!" he shouted: "Damn you, you stinking brutes!"

He fired the revolver again, and the sound of the shot echoed hollowly, the bullet whining as it ricocheted from metal to metal. He emptied the cylinder, cursing the rats as he did so. "Damn you! Damn you! Damn you!"

When the hammer clicked he drew back from the hole. His hands were shaking and his head ached. He took the revolver back to the cabin, put it away in the drawer, and lay down on the settee.

The day passed without incident on board the *Hopeful Enterprise*. She was still listing slightly, but the list did not appear to have got any worse. The weather was being kind and the engines were on their best behaviour, so that by nightfall the ship was a good hundred miles east of the spot where the *India Star* had been recovered.

Barling knew, however, that it was too early for any complacency. There were still between seven and eight hundred miles of ocean to be passed, and even if all went well that meant another nine or ten days of steaming at the speed they were making. In that time all kinds of undesirable things might happen, and he was very much aware of the tug, never far away, prepared to take advantage of any mishap. He would not be able to relax until both ships were safe in harbour.

Madden, too, was still worrying. The engines had been patched up once, but he was far from confident that they would not break down again. He confided his fears to Loder, but got little encouragement in that quarter. The mate was in one of his sardonic moods and seemed to take a mischievous pleasure in depressing the chief engineer's spirits even more.

"You'd better keep that heap of old scrap-iron working.

If not, we're going to be in trouble with our tow. We might have to turn it over to the tug. They'd be pleased."

" Barling wouldn't do that."

" He might have no alternative. You can't tow another ship if your own is incapable of pushing herself."

Madden looked gloomy. " If we hand over to the tug there'll be no salvage money."

" Unless they feel like giving us a share—for our good work. Which is about as likely as a heat wave at the South Pole. And if we lose the salvage money you know what happens."

Madden's troubled eyes searched Loder's face for any spark of comfort, and could find none. " You really believe B. and C. will go into liquidation?"

Loder put a hand on Madden's shoulder and gave his most malicious grin. " I'm sure of it, Chief. Dead sure."

" Oh, God!"

" And it's no use appealing to God. He won't help you. You've just got to help yourself. It's up to you to keep the wheels turning."

" I may not be able to do that."

" If you don't you'll be looking for a new job."

Madden sighed heavily. Loder gave him a parting slap on the shoulder and walked away. Madden watched him go and regretted having broached the subject; he ought to have known that he would get little cheer from the mate.

It was after midnight, but Wilson had not been to sleep although he was lying in a comfortable bunk. And he was not at all certain that he wanted to sleep, tired though he was; when he slept he had too many nightmares and woke sweating and screaming.

He was in a state midway between dozing and waking

when he heard the stutter of a petrol engine, and he was not sure at first whether it was real or merely part of a dream. But the sound persisted and grew louder, and Wilson became fully awake with the realisation that a boat must be approaching the *India Star*. His immediate thought was that it must be from the *Hopeful Enterprise*, but a moment's reflection convinced him that it was far more likely to be from the *Atlantic Scavenger*.

There was an emergency battery-operated light in the cabin, but Wilson did not switch it on. He slipped out of the bunk, groped for his trousers and pulled them on. He found his thick seaman's jersey, and was pulling that on too when he heard the boat thump against the side of the ship, and the sound of the engine died away. He thrust his feet into gumboots and went into the day cabin. It was not completely dark, for the moon had risen and some light was coming in through the scuttle. Wilson crossed to the desk, pulled out the drawer where the revolver was, loaded it quickly, and made his way up to the port wing of the bridge.

It was a clear, cold night, and the ship was bathed in pale moonlight. There was very little wind and the sea was smoother than it had been earlier. The silvery light gave to everything a kind of enchanted appearance, like a scene out of some fairy tale, and a few hundred yards ahead Wilson could see the blunt outline of the *Hopeful Enterprise* with the light at her stern. Not far off on the port beam was the tug.

Then he saw the men come up over the bulwark, and he knew that this was a take-over bid. He thought for a moment that the tow-rope must have parted, leaving the *India Star* ripe for the picking, but almost immediately he knew that this could not be so, since she was still moving forward. So there could be only one explanation: the master of the *Atlantic Scavenger* had become tired of waiting for the

prize to fall into his lap and had decided to take more
positive action. And any remaining doubts that Wilson
might have had on this point were dispelled when he saw
that the four men who had climbed on board the *India Star*
were heading for the forecastle and that one of them was
carrying an implement that looked remarkably like an axe.

Wilson, still with the revolver gripped in his right hand,
descended the ladders from the bridge to the foredeck and
ran towards the forecastle. By the time he reached the head
of the forecastle ladder the four men were grouped by the
bollards to which the towing-hawser was belayed. They
had their backs to Wilson, and apparently had been unaware
of his approach. He stepped off the top rung of the ladder
and paused with his left hand on the rail. He could hear the
subdued mutter of the men's voices but was unable to catch
what they were saying. Then one of them laughed—the big
man who was carrying the axe—and the others backed away
a pace or two to give him room. The big man raised the
axe above his head, and it was obvious that his purpose was
to cut through the hawser.

" Stop!" Wilson said.

The man lowered the axe and wheeled round. The other
three turned also, and for a moment the face of one of them
was caught in the moonlight. Wilson recognised him from a
previous encounter: it was the mate of the *Atlantic
Scavenger*, the man who had introduced himself as Creegan.

" Well, now," Creegan said. " Look who's here."

" Get off this ship," Wilson said.

They all laughed: It seemed to amuse them. Wilson did
not share the amusement; he was dead serious. He was
angry too; he resented this intrusion on his privacy. This
was his ship and they had no right to be there. But they were
making no move to obey him.

"Did you hear me?"

"Oh, we heard you, sonny," Creegan said. "But we just don't feel inclined to go. We've got a job to do." He did not show any great surprise at seeing Wilson; he had, of course, been aware that there was a man on board.

"You've got no job to do here. You've got no business aboard this ship."

"Oh, but we have," Creegan said. He had a soft, not unpleasant voice, with an almost singing intonation. "And when we've finished we're going to take you back with us to the tug."

"And suppose I don't want to go?"

"Oh, but you will. It'll be to your advantage. Very much so."

Wilson began to get the drift of it. They were going to pay him to betray Captain Barling. Then they could say he had voluntarily left the *India Star* and that the ship had been drifting and abandoned when they had taken it in tow. That would take care of the legal point, and no one could prove that they had cut the tow-rope.

"Are you offering me a bribe?"

"Bribe!" Creegan said in that gentle, singing voice. "Now who's talking about bribes? Let's just say we could make it worth your while to row in with us."

"And if I refuse?"

The other three men laughed again, especially the one with the axe.

Creegan said: "It's a big ocean. Men fall overboard. They don't often come out alive."

There was the threat as an alternative, the carrot and the whip; it was for him to choose. And he did not doubt that the threat was real, that it was no bluff. There was a lot of money at stake and these were hard men, however soft and gentle Creegan's voice might be. Perhaps he was the hardest of them all.

Anger flared up in Wilson. What made them think they could manipulate him like this? It was an insult.

" Get off my ship."

That really amused them; their laughter jarred on Wilson's hearing; the big man was almost doubled up.

" Your ship?" Creegan said. " That's rich, that is. And who gave it to you, for Pete's sake?"

" I'm in charge here." Wilson was conscious that his voice was rising almost to a squeak, try though he might to control it. Who were they to laugh at him? " I'm telling you for the last time: get off my ship."

Creegan was losing patience. " That's enough, sonny. You've had your joke. Now let's get on with it. Paddy, cut that hawser."

The man called Paddy lifted his axe. Wilson darted forward and got the windlass between himself and the four men. He rested his arms on the windlass, gripped the revolver in both hands and pointed it at Paddy.

" Stop, or I'll kill you!"

Something in Wilson's voice made the big man stop again. He turned to face Wilson, and saw the revolver.

" Bejasus, he's got a gun!"

None of them had noticed it before. They all stared at it, not moving.

" Now," Creegan said, speaking slowly and carefully, " don't do anything silly. We know you wouldn't really shoot. You're just fooling. Maybe you'd better give me that gun." He took a cautious step towards Wilson and stopped as the barrel of the revolver moved to cover him.

" Come any nearer," Wilson said, " and you'll see if I'll really shoot."

Creegan hesitated. " I don't believe it's loaded," he said; he sounded none too sure of it.

Wilson said nothing. He could hear the faint slap of water against the bows and the sound of the motor-boat bumping against the side as it was dragged along by the ship. There was moisture on the iron of the windlass and he could feel the chill of it through the sleeves of his jersey.

The three other men were looking to Creegan to make the first move. He had to do something or admit defeat. He took another step forward. Wilson aimed low and fired.

It was impossible to tell where the bullet went, but the screech of the ricochet indicated that it had struck the deck, possibly quite close to Creegan's feet. He jumped back as though he had trodden on a snake.

" Now do you believe it's loaded?"

" You're crazy," Creegan said. " You might have killed me."

" So I might. And if you don't get to hell out of it I might still do just that. Now are you going?"

It was the big man who broke first. " Sure an' I'm not standing here to be shot at by a nutter. I'm away back to the boat." He walked to the ladder and went down it quickly, as though fearful of a shot in the back. He was still carrying the axe.

It was the signal for a general retirement. The two who had said nothing suddenly decided to follow the big man. They walked away hurriedly and were jammed briefly at the head of the ladder; then they were gone.

Wilson made a gesture with the revolver. " Now you."

Creegan seemed to be choking. " You'll pay for this. It's —it's illegal. It's—"

Wilson fired again, to the right of Creegan. It was enough for the mate of the *Atlantic Scavenger*; he turned and ran.

Wilson emptied the revolver, spraying the shots wildly. By the time he had finished Creegan was already scrambling over the bulwark. Wilson stuck the revolver in his belt and followed at a more leisurely pace.

When he reached the place where the Jacob's-ladder was still dangling over the side the men in the boat had cast off and had started the engine. The boat dropped astern of the *India Star* and headed back towards the tug. Wilson rested his elbows on the bulwark and watched it go. Then he reached down and began hauling in the Jacob's-ladder. He did not think the men would try again, but if they did they would not find it so easy to get on board a second time.

The encounter with the boarding party had given Wilson a feeling of exhilaration. He had driven them off; it had been one against four and he had mastered them; he had proved himself equal to the emergency. He really was master of this ship; he and he alone.

But the brief elation had already begun to subside even before he got back to the cabin; and when he lay down again on the bunk it had given way to a mood of black depression. What was it to him that the boarders had been repulsed? He had another, heavier matter on his mind, and that was something you could not drive away with a gun; something that nothing could drive away; something that would be with him as long as he lived.

He buried his face in the pillow and groaned.

THIRTEEN

RUSSIAN ROULETTE

THE LOOKOUT on the poop of the *Hopeful Enterprise* had neither seen nor heard anything of what was happening on board the *India Star*. He had seen the lights of the tug and had remarked to himself that they seemed to be rather closer than usual, but had thought nothing of it. Once or twice he had detected something that might have been the faint sound of a motor-boat, but he could not see one and had come to the conclusion that he must have imagined it. The *India Star* was just a dark shape in the moonlight and the tow seemed to be going well. At the end of his spell on watch he reported nothing unusual and went off to his bunk to sleep far more soundly than Wilson was able to do in considerably more luxurious quarters.

As daylight spread over a cold, grey sea, Captain Barling was pleased to see the other ship still following astern, still joined by the long tow-rope to the *Hopeful Enterprise*. One more night had passed without mishap; a few more miles had been lopped off the total; the odds against the venture's succeeding had been slightly reduced. It was something.

Scotton came to him, again bubbling with excitement. "It's getting to be a big story, sir. Really big."

Barling looked at him with raised eyebrows. "What is?"

" This." Scotton's right hand made a flapping motion. " This operation."

" You make it sound like something surgical. But I take it that you mean this towing job."

" Yes, sir." Scotton sounded a little impatient. What else did the Old Man think he could have meant? " Seems it's caught the imagination of the British public. The newspapers are blowing it up for all they're worth. They're calling it a tense drama of the sea."

" They would," Barling said disgustedly. He was none too pleased about the publicity; all that ballyhoo. It meant that there would be no chance now of slipping in quietly without fuss, as he had originally hoped to do. And of course Bruce Calthorp would have heard about it; couldn't help doing so. He wondered what Calthorp was thinking; whether he would guess the reason for his partner's action, guess that this was snatching at a straw. Probably. But it made no difference.

" There seems to be some argument going on about the legal situation, sir. I mean about whether you were acting within your rights in preventing the tug's crew going on board the *India Star*."

" Did you put that story out?" Barling asked sharply.

" No, sir." Scotton was quick to disown responsibility. " It must have come from the tug."

" H'm!" Barling gave Scotton a long, searching look before apparently accepting the truth of this statement. " And what seems to be the general opinion on that point?"

" That the action was legal, sir, if our men were in fact first on board."

" If! There can't be any doubt about that."

" We can't have any doubt about it, sir, I agree. But

people who were not present might have if the skipper of the
tug were to put out a different version."

" He'd never get away with it."

" I hope not, sir."

Barling hoped so too. The possibility had not crossed
his mind until then, and it did not please him. He saw a
possibly long drawn out legal dispute ahead even if they got
the *India Star* in. It was just one more thing to worry about.
Damn the tug! Why did it have to turn up? And just at the
wrong moment.

" It seems," Scotton went on, " that the journalists are
making Charlie Wilson into something of a national hero."

" Hero?"

" Well, it's the sort of thing they love, isn't it? Young
seaman alone on ship of death. Makes a good headline."

" Balderdash!"

" It's what people like, sir. I think Wilson's in for a big
welcome when he steps ashore. Could be on television and
all that."

Barling gave Scotton a sudden hard stare. " How did they
get hold of his name? Did you tell them that?"

Scotton shifted uneasily. " Well, sir, you did say there was
no reason to keep radio silence any longer."

" I didn't tell you to set up as a gossip column of the air."

" I'm sorry, sir. Of course, if I'd known. But I don't see
what harm there can be in it."

" Harm!" Barling said, and then stopped. Scotton was
probably right. The news was out now, and there was no
point in trying to hide any part of it. So why not let young
Wilson have his glory? " Very well, Sparks; very well."

Wilson himself, alone on board the *India Star,* was unaware
that his name was in the news, that indeed he had become a

popular hero. And if the newsmen had known that he had repulsed a nocturnal attempt to take over the ship by firing a revolver at the boarders, his heroism might have been blown up to an even greater size. But that was an incident that was unlikely to be revealed over the tug's radio and was unknown to anyone in the *Hopeful Enterprise*. However, even without that titbit, the affair was intriguing enough to stay in the forefront of the news; the uncertainty regarding the outcome was a guarantee that interest would not slacken, and some of the big betting firms had even opened books on the result.

The struggle of the three ships far out in the Atlantic was a story that could not be allowed to die until it had reached its conclusion. And what that conclusion might be was anybody's guess, depending as it did on so many imponderables: the engines of the *Hopeful Enterprise*, the strength of the tow-rope, the buoyancy of the *India Star* and, above all, the weather. It was the weather that might have the last word.

Wilson had had a bad night. He had slept a while, but the sleep had done him little good, for it had brought the most terrible nightmares. Again he was strangling the woman, but she would not die. His hands were at her throat and she was laughing in his face, laughing, laughing, laughing, as if in mockery of his futile efforts to kill her. He squeezed more tightly, but the neck was too big; his fingers could not encompass it; it was fat and slimy, so that he could not get a grip on it. He was cursing the woman, cursing and weeping; he had to kill her, though he did not know why; he just knew that he had to.

Then, suddenly, the flesh seemed to melt away in his hands and he was holding only bone, a skeleton, the empty sockets of the skull staring at him, the mouth still wide, still with the mocking laughter coming from it. And then the arms of the skeleton were round him, drawing him close, and the mouth was coming towards his lips in the travesty of a kiss. He turned his head away, struggling to free himself from that ghastly embrace, and awoke drenched in sweat, and screaming.

He slept no more, but lay there in the darkness waiting for the day to come.

They saw him from the *Hopeful Enterprise* moving about the ship, on the bridge, on the forecastle. He made no signal to them, and they assumed that all was well with him. They knew nothing of the turmoil in his mind, the torment that never left him now. He was a hero, wasn't he? What had he to worry about?

The hero sat that evening in the captain's cabin, held the revolver to his head and squeezed the trigger. There was a metallic click as the hammer fell on an empty chamber. He lowered the revolver and let it rest in his lap. He had won again. Or had he lost? What stake was he playing for? Life or death? Even he could not answer that question.

After a while he picked up the revolver again and twirled the cylinder. There was one round in it; one loaded chamber and five empty ones; one chance in six of death, five of life. Perhaps he had made the odds too great; perhaps later he would make them more even; another round in the cylinder; two more.

He pressed the cold muzzle against his right temple, his index finger tightening on the trigger. Once more the hammer tripped forward with a dull click.

Wilson lowered the gun with a shaking hand. There was sweat on his brow and his head throbbed. He stood up, put the revolver away in its drawer, then walked to the settee and lay down. The thudding inside his head was almost unbearable. There was a shaft of sunlight coming through the scuttle. He watched it moving as the ship rolled.

On the fourth day the engines of the *Hopeful Enterprise* broke down again. Both freighters drifted, rolling in the swell, and the gap between them narrowed. The slack in the towing-hawser was winched in and Captain Barling looked with misgiving at the bows of the *India Star*. There could be trouble if the two ships came together.

The tug moved in close and her master addressed Barling through a loud-hailer. " You want some help, Captain?" The mockery in the question was not even veiled.

Barling replied briefly that he did not.

" We could maybe take the pair of ye in tow. Just say the word."

Barling declined to say the word. Every man in the tug seemed to be on deck and looking towards the *Hopeful Enterprise*. Mr. Loder, observing with his binoculars, could see that most of them were grinning. Obviously they thought the prize was going to fall into their hands now.

" No! To hell with that!" Loder muttered. " They're not having it now. Not after all we've done. Damn those engines!"

Madden was damning them too; toiling in his oily dungeon below decks with the other engineers. He knew how much depended on getting the machinery moving again, the great shaft revolving. His whole future depended on it. He drove himself and he drove the others. They were surprised; they had never known the chief to be so tough, to snarl at them with such ferocity. They were a trifle awed too; it was as though they had discovered that what they had always supposed to be a St. Bernard had suddenly become a wolf.

The second steward, looking in on his patient, found Trubshaw in low spirits.

"We've broken down again," Trubshaw said. "Well, what did they expeck, towin' that other bleedin' ship? Now maybe they'll let the tug take 'er. Should've done in the first place."

Tricker shook his head. "We're not letting her go yet. While there's any chance of hanging on to her you can bet your boots the Old Man's going to hang on."

Trubshaw groaned. "The bastard's crazy. An' I'll tell you what—'e's killin' me. 'E don't care a damn abaht me. 'E's jus' goin' to let me die."

"If you're going to die," Tricker said with a sly glance at Trubshaw's pale, unshaven face, "I don't see how the Old Man can stop you. He's not God."

Trubshaw looked venomous. "You know what I mean. I oughter be 'ome, in 'ospital. An' 'ere we are, 'angin' arahnd arter this bleedin' tow-rope job. It's bleedin' madness."

"I like the madness," Tricker said softly, and began straightening the covers on Trubshaw's bunk. "We could all get something out of it."

"All I'll get's a bleedin' coffin."

"If you die at sea," Tricker said, "you may have to make do with a few yards of canvas."

He went away silently on rubber-soled shoes, leaving Trubshaw to think about being sewn up in a few yards of sail-cloth.

As the *Hopeful Enterprise* rose and fell, rolling a little, her engines silent, the two ships drifted gradually closer together. Wilson went up on to the forecastle of the *India*

Star and gazed across the narrowing gap. He could see Mr. Loder and the bosun and a few seamen clustered at the stern of the *Hopeful Enterprise* and working on the hawser. Eventually the distance shrank so much that it was possible to shout across from one ship to the other. He heard the mate's voice and was just able to catch the words.

" Are you all right, Wilson?"

Wilson made a megaphone with his hands and shouted back. " I'm all right."

" Got all you need?"

" Yes. Everything."

" You're happy where you are then?"

What a question that was! Happy! As if he could ever be happy again! Could a haunted man be happy?

But he shouted a second time: " I'm all right."

Loder was satisfied. He had other things to worry about, chief of which was the possibility of the *India Star* ramming the stern of the *Hopeful Enterprise* or drifting ahead. With the same forces acting on both vessels, it might have been expected that they would remain in the same relative positions; but this was not so; slowly but inevitably they were closing with each other while the crew of the tug looked on, waiting and hoping.

" Come on, Jonah, come on," Loder muttered. " Get them moving, can't you?"

As if in answer, he heard the sound he had been waiting for. Madden had done it again: the engines had come to life.

" Good for him," Rankin said. " Now we're on our way."

They paid out the hawser again and the gap widened. The tug, robbed once more of its prize, drew away, and Wilson left the forecastle of the *India Star*. The towing job settled down into the old pattern.

On the sixth day the weather turned on them: the wind strengthened, there was rain and there was sleet, and the sea was troubled. The decks of the *Hopeful Enterprise* ran with water as she ploughed heavily on with spray bursting over her forecastle. Even more disturbing, the list to port had perceptibly increased; as the ship rolled she was dipping far deeper on her port than on her starboard side, and that was something Captain Barling did not at all like to see.

Loder was characteristically gloomy. " We didn't want this just now. We'd be in trouble even without that load on our tail."

Barling said acidly: " Are you suggesting we should cut the tow?"

Loder seemed surprised at the question. " Cut the tow! Lord, no. After all we've done we don't want to let go now."

" So you've changed your mind? You think we've got a chance?"

Loder grinned suddenly, and it was a genuine grin, without a trace of cynicism or mockery. It was friendly, even a shade conspiratorial; it seemed to say that they were in this together, both with the same object in view, partners. It surprised Barling, but the surprise was a pleasant one.

" We'll make the chance. That tug can go to blazes. No one is going to take our prize."

" Well," Barling said, " I'm glad to see that you're on my side."

Loder glanced towards the tug and shrugged. " In the face of the common enemy you have to stick together. Isn't that so?"

Barling nodded. " Yes, I suppose it is."

But by nightfall the prospects were not looking at all bright. The wind had got itself round into the south-west and was leaning heavily on the ships. The seaman on taff-rail watch on board the *Hopeful Enterprise*, remembering what had happened to Trubshaw, looked warily at the hawser, waiting for any sign that it might be about to break and ready to take avoiding action, while nearly a quarter of a mile astern Wilson braced himself against the plunging of the *India Star* and listened to the seas beating against the side.

For Wilson the ship was haunted. It was the ghost of the dead woman. Waking or sleeping, she haunted him now; he could never rid his mind of that ghastly phantom. He feared for his sanity. Was the strain driving him mad? The idea of madness seemed more dreadful than anything else. It could not be; he would not accept it. And yet, what could these phantoms be but the imaginings of a sick mind?

" No," he muttered. " Not that, not that! "

He went out on to the wing of the bridge. The moon and the stars were blotted out by a heavy blanket of cloud and the wind tore at him out of the darkness, driving the rain into his face. He gripped the rail and let the wind and the rain hit him, accepting the blows. He looked down and saw a glimmer of foam where the water slid past the ship's side or beat against it, flinging up spray. The deck moved shudderingly under his feet, and he thought: Now! I could end it! He had only to climb over the rail and fall into the darkness.

But after a while he went back into the cabin, drenched and shivering. He switched the light on and took the revolver from the drawer. He loaded three rounds into the cylinder, so that there were three full chambers and three empty, evenly spaced. He sat down on the settee and twirled the cylinder. He pressed the muzzle of the revolver to his temple and placed his finger on the trigger. He was shivering so violently that he could not hold the gun steady. He grasped his right wrist with his left hand to stop it shaking. And still he hesitated to press the trigger. The chances of death were one in two; he was as likely to spatter his brains against the bulkhead as he was to survive. The wheel was no longer weighted one way or the other; it was evenly balanced.

The ship rolled heavily and the revolver barrel slipped away from his head. He fell over on to his side and heard the wind howling. A chair slid a little way and stopped. Wilson straightened up and once again put the gun to his head. He took a deep breath and squeezed the trigger.

Something seemed to burst inside his head. He gave a cry, as though of pain. But there was no pain. He was trembling uncontrollably and, cold as he was, there was sweat on his forehead. He looked at the revolver, hardly able to believe that it had not fired. Yet it was so. He pulled back the hammer and saw that once again it had fallen on an empty chamber.

He lay back on the settee, breathing deeply, his heart thudding. He had no idea how long he stayed thus; it could have been five minutes, it could have been an hour. Then he sat up once more, twirled the cylinder, and once more pressed the muzzle against his temple.

His mouth was dry, his throat parched, his breathing quick and shallow. He hesitated with his finger on the trigger, unable to bring himself to go through with it a second time. It was scarcely conceivable that the hammer would again come down on an empty chamber; this time when he squeezed the trigger he would surely blast himself out of life. And what of that? What if he did? It would be a release from the torment he was enduring. He could not go on living as things were; life for him had become unbearable.

He clenched his teeth and gradually increased the pressure

of his finger on the trigger. Suddenly the hammer tripped forward, but again there was nothing but a metallic click; no bullet driving into his brain. He was still alive; he could not even kill himself.

He examined the revolver and saw that the hammer had in fact struck the base of a round, and the round had misfired. It was one chance in a thousand, in ten thousand. He shuddered. Was he not to be allowed to die? Was this part of his punishment—that he was condemned to live on with his torment? With a cry of despair he rushed from the cabin and out on to the open deck, the revolver still in his hand. The rain lashed at him but he ignored it. He groped his way to the rail and flung the revolver far out into the darkness. He did not hear it drop into the sea; he heard the shrill piping of the wind and the thunder of the waves, and that was all.

FOURTEEN

HAWSER

MORNING CAME with the *Hopeful Enterprise* still linked to the *India Star* by the long tow-rope. The wind was blowing from the south-west but not with quite the force it had had the previous day. Indeed, if it had not been for the increased list to port, Barling might have been feeling reasonably happy about the state of affairs. Though there was also the rather disturbing fact that the *Hopeful Enterprise* was definitely lower by the head; there was some water getting in somewhere which the pumps seemed incapable of clearing. That, combined with the list, made him more than a little worried.

He had in his time sailed in ships in much worse condition, but they had not had uncertain engines and they had not been towing other ships; above all, his fortunes had not been completely dependant on them as they were on the *Hopeful Enterprise*. If he failed to bring the *India Star* into port he was finished. But suppose he lost both ships. That possibility hardly bore thinking about; and yet it persisted at the back of his mind, plaguing him.

Scotton, bringing further reports of continuing public interest in the story, was almost unbearably cheerful.

" We're in for a great welcome when we get home, sir."

Barling answered sourly: " We're not there yet."

Scotton, undeterred, went on: " The odds have shortened on the betting market. Quite a lot."

" The betting market! What in hell do bookies know about it? They aren't out here, are they? They don't know what it's like. Don't talk to me about odds. I know what the odds are."

" Yes, sir." Scotton sounded a shade less effervescent. " Still, we have got as far as this, sir; so there seems no reason why we shouldn't finish the job."

" No reason! There are a thousand reasons."

" But we'll do it, sir. We'll do it."

Barling could see that Scotton really believed that. The radio officer was young and enthusiastic. Barling felt a certain contempt for him: that silly beard, which was no proper beard at all, ought to be shaved off; it looked ridiculous.

" You've got a lot of confidence. I'm not sure it's altogether warranted."

Scotton looked at Barling, his eyes shining. " I've got confidence in you, sir. You'll see it through."

Barling was startled. What was this? Hero worship? He would not have supposed himself capable of inspiring anything of that kind in anyone. He felt very far from heroic. Yet apparently young Scotton had trust in him; looked on him perhaps as some kind of superman. Amazing. But in spite of himself he felt a certain glow around the heart. Perhaps if Scotton believed in him others did too: Walpole, Thompson, Madden; possibly even Loder. But no; that was going a little too far; Loder believed in no one but himself. Nevertheless . . .

He became aware that Scotton was still gazing at him, still with that look in his eyes. Barling said gruffly: " I can't promise anything. We'll need a sack of luck to get through."

" You'll do it, sir," Scotton said. " You'll do it."

Going into the wheelhouse, Barling found the third mate
on watch.

" Well?" Barling said. " What do you think?"

" Think, sir? About what?"

" About our chances. Shall we do it?"

" I'm sure we shall, sir."

" Dammit!" Barling said. " You don't have to say that.
Look out there." He pointed at the foredeck, visible through
the wheelhouse windows, the list only too apparent, seas
spilling over the bulwarks. " Does that look as though we'll
make it? Tell the truth, man."

" I am telling the truth, sir." Walpole was insistent. " I
still think we'll make it. And Mr. Thompson does too."

" Did he tell you that?"

" Yes, sir. He said you were determined to take the *India
Star* in, and you damned well would, come hell or high
water. Those were his words, sir."

Barling stared at Walpole so long and so fixedly that the
young man became uneasy and looked away. Finally Barling gave a shrug and turned away also. They were crazy, all
of them, but he was glad.

The tug was still there. It was like a gadfly; you might
flap it away but always it came back. It was the threat, the
visual reminder that they had only to falter and the prize
might yet be snatched from them; that all their labour, all
their endeavour, might still come to nothing.

" Once," Loder remarked to Barling, " there was a four-
inch gun on the poop. I'm rather sorry it's not there now."

Barling could not be certain whether Loder was joking or
serious. If the gun had still been there he might really have

used it, if only as a warning. That was the kind of man he was.

"They won't leave us as long as they think they've got the least chance. They've invested time and money in this too. They'll want to get it back."

He could see their point of view. In their place he would probably have done the same.

"They'll get nothing," Loder said. "Nothing."

Wilson felt as though he had a fever. His head seemed to have a fire burning inside it. He had not changed his wet clothes but had allowed them to dry on him. His bones ached and he had uncontrollable bouts of shivering. For most of the day he lay on the settee. He ate scarcely anything, but occasionally he made himself a hot drink and swallowed it with some discomfort because of the soreness in his throat. Once or twice he ventured out on to the wing of the bridge and was seen from the *Hopeful Enterprise*, but he did not go up to the forecastle.

Orwell, in between his normal duties, found time to visit Trubshaw. He found Trubshaw in low spirits, which pleased him. Orwell was not the kind of man to forget and forgive, and he had not forgotten that Trubshaw had tried to kill him; nor had he forgiven. His purpose, therefore, in visiting the invalid was not to offer consolation but rather to enjoy the spectacle of Trubshaw suffering.

"Well," Orwell said, "I see you're still alive."

Trubshaw scowled at him. "No thanks to that bastard up on the bridge."

"You think you're going to die?" Orwell asked softly, watching Trubshaw through the wreaths of smoke from his pipe.

Trubshaw winced with pain as he turned his head on the pillow. " I'm a sick man. You can see that, carncher? An' I'm gettin' worse."

" You do look pretty sick," Orwell admitted. " I remember a man as looked like you, years ago it was, on the long Pacific run from Panama to Wellington. Got a knock on the head from a fall on deck."

" What 'appened to 'im?" Trubshaw's gaze was fixed on Orwell's face and there was fear in his eyes. " Did 'e—"

Orwell sucked complacently at his pipe. " He hung on for a while, looking sick, moaning about the pain. Yes, he hung on for quite a while—a week, ten days, maybe."

" An' then?"

" He died."

" Oh, Gawd!"

" There was no doctor on board, you see, and it was a long voyage. I daresay he'd have been all right if we could have got him to hospital, but we couldn't. So he got worse and worse, and finally he died. Steward went in to look at him one morning and there he was—stiff."

Trubshaw's face was pallid, his eyes wide. Orwell tamped the burning tobacco in his pipe with a horny thumb and looked at him without pity.

" Could be the way they'll find you, Trub. Some fine morning. Soon."

" Get aht of 'ere," Trubshaw said in a low, hoarse voice. " Get aht of 'ere an' leave me alone, damn yer!"

Orwell stood up. " If that's what you want, Trub. I just thought you'd be glad of a bit of company. Most people are—in their last hours."

The day passed slowly; a grey, depressing day with intermittent rain, thin and cold, and no sun. The wind moderated and veered a little, getting more into the west. The sea became appreciably calmer, and the two ships ploughed on, eating away at the miles separating them from their landfall.

The list to port of the *Hopeful Enterprise* gave the decks a permanent slope. The tug again came in close and her master repeated his offer of help.

" You're in trouble, Captain. Your ship's in bad shape."

" She's well enough."

" Ye'll never make it, Captain. Be sensible now. Let us take over."

" Go home," Barling shouted. " There's nothing for you here."

He heard a ragged cheer, and looking down saw half the crew of the *Hopeful Enterprise* lining the bulwarks. It was obvious that they had heard his words and were in agreement with them. Once again Barling felt a sudden warming of the heart; it was good to know that he had the men with him.

The tug sheered off, speeded on its way by catcalls and rude gestures from the *Hopeful Enterprise*. But it did not go far. There were many miles still lying ahead and the prize might still fall from hands that had become too weak to hold it. When that happened the tug would be there.

The next day Wilson was still slightly feverish, but his appetite had returned. He cooked a breakfast and ate ravenously; then, for the first time in two days, he went up to the forecastle and examined the hawser. What he saw was in no way reassuring. Where the hawser passed through the fairlead there had been considerable chafing and some of the strands of wire were already worn through. Indeed, it was only too apparent that it was simply a question of time —and not very much time at that—before the hawser broke altogether, leaving the *India Star* once again adrift. It could happen that day; it could happen in the night; and then if the tugmen came again how could he drive them away without a revolver?

Wilson looked at the hawser. It was creaking slightly where it ran through the fairlead, but the sea was smoother now and the ship was rolling only a little. But what could he do? He knew what needed to be done: a few feet of the tow-rope needed to be drawn in so that the weak portion was no longer taking the strain. But though it was easy enough to see what ought to be done, how to do it was quite another question. And then he remembered what Mr. Loder had said about signalling if he needed help. Well, he needed help now, so he had better get on with it.

He ran back to the bridge and found a signalling flag, carried it up to the forecastle and started waving it from side to side. For a time there was no response from the other ship. Could it be that no one on board the *Hopeful Enterprise* was keeping a watch on the tow? In a fit of petulance at this apparent neglect Wilson lowered the flag and was in half a mind to go away and leave the hawser to take its chance. But he decided that this would be a childish thing to do; he lifted the flag and started signalling again.

Ten minutes later he saw a boat being lowered from the *Hopeful Enterprise* and shortly afterwards it was on its way. The *Hopeful Enterprise* had stopped to lower the boat; she had turned slightly broadside on as she lost steerage way and the strain was off the hawser.

The boat soon reached the *India Star*; it was the one with the motor in it, and somebody had apparently done some work on the engine, for it was working again. Wilson went down to the foredeck to put the Jacob's-ladder over the side and take the painter.

It was Mr. Loder who stepped on board and he had his usual crew with the addition of an extra hand.

" Well," he said as soon as he climbed over the bulwark, " what's the trouble?"

Wilson told him. He led the way to the forecastle and showed Loder.

" I couldn't do anything about it, sir. Not on my own."

" Of course not," Loder said. " But we can."

He gave brisk orders and the men got to work at once. In a very short time enough of the hawser had been hauled in to carry the chafed portion clear of any strain. Then it was belayed again to the bollards.

" It'll be all right now," Loder said. He turned and stared hard at Wilson. " You don't look well; not at all well. Are you feeling ill?"

" No," Wilson said. " There's nothing wrong with me."

Loder seemed unconvinced. " I'm not so sure. Maybe it's being here on your own that's getting you down."

" Nothing's getting me down."

" All the same I think you'd better come back with us."

Wilson refused with a vehemence that surprised Loder. " No, I don't want to. I'd rather stay here. I'm needed here."

" It's not essential."

" If I hadn't been here," Wilson said, " we'd have lost this ship."

Loder had to admit the possibility. " Though we can't be absolutely certain about that. The hawser might have held in spite of the chafing."

" I didn't mean that," Wilson said.

" What did you mean?"

But Wilson would say no more. He did not wish to talk about his encounter with the boarding party from the tug, about the way in which he had driven them off by shooting

at them with a revolver. Least of all did he wish to speak
about the revolver. Orwell, Lawson and Veevers might have
admired him for what he had done; even Mr. Loder might
have done so. He did not wish to be admired; he simply
wanted to be left alone. There were other things he could
not tell them about; things that had to remain secret, buried
deeply in his own mind. He had thrown the revolver into
the sea, but the dark and bitter memory of what had happened in Montreal could not be so easily cast away; it
remained to torment him. Waking or sleeping, it tormented
him still. And of that he could tell no one.

" You're sure you want to stay?" Loder said.

" Yes, I'm sure."

Orwell said: " I think Mr. Loder's right. I think you look
sick."

" I'm not sick. Just leave me alone, that's all I ask."

" Well," Loder said at last, " if that's the way you feel
we'll be getting back."

" It is the way I feel," Wilson said.

He watched the boat returning to the *Hopeful Enterprise*;
he waited on the forecastle until the strain had been taken
up by the hawser; then he went back to the bridge.

Though he did not know it, he had effectively killed the
last chance the master of the *Atlantic Scavenger* might have
had of snatching the *India Star* for himself. From that
moment the prize was undoubtedly Barling's.

FIFTEEN

LAST HOLD

THE SEA-GOING launch had come a long way to meet them. It was an old naval torpedo boat and it appeared early in the forenoon watch when Barling was on the bridge with the third mate. Barling did not at first realise that the launch had come out to meet the *Hopeful Enterprise*; he thought it was perhaps on a fishing trip.

During the last few days all had gone remarkably smoothly: the list had not increased, the weather had been surprisingly good, and the tow-rope had held. Barling felt grateful to Charlie Wilson for what he had done; yet he was still unaware of quite how much he owed the young seaman. He knew nothing of the repulse, of the boarding party from the tug; he did not know that, but for Wilson's resourceful action in that instance, the *India Star* would most certainly not still have been hanging on to the tail of the *Hopeful Enterprise*.

For Barling had no means of knowing about that; he knew only of the work that had been done on board his own ship, work that he imagined had been solely responsible for the success of the towing operation. And that it was a success could no longer be doubted. Even the master of the tug had at last accepted the fact and had given up shadowing the other two ships. That morning they had looked for the *Atlantic Scavenger* in vain: she had gone home.

"That launch," Walpole remarked suddenly, "is heading our way, sir."

Barling had already come to the same conclusion. The launch was not only coming towards them; it was moving fast. If the *Hopeful Enterprise* and her tow had been able to make that kind of speed they would have been in harbour days ago.

He wondered what the business of the launch could be, but on that point at least he was not to be left long in doubt. The launch turned in a wide curve and drew abreast of the *Hopeful Enterprise* on the starboard side, cutting its speed to match that of the ship.

There were several men standing on the deck of the launch. One of them, a tall man wearing a sheepskin coat and a check cap, shouted: "Ahoy there! Can I come on board?"

Barling looked down at him from the wing of the bridge. "Who are you?"

"Peter Wayne. *Sunday Record.* I'd like an interview, Captain."

"I've got a job to do," Barling said curtly. "I've no time for interviews."

Wayne grinned. "And a grand job too. My congratulations. That's why the *Record* would like your personal story. Exclusive. Be worth your while. It's a wealthy paper."

Barling thought it over. He detested the ballyhoo of the newspaper world and hated the idea of figuring in some blown-up story for people to read over their Sunday breakfast. But whether he liked it or not, he was already in the news and there was no possibility of avoiding publicity now. So why not make the best of a bad job and strike a bargain with the *Record*? Money was money, however you made it; and money was something he badly needed.

" All right, Mr. Wayne. You may come aboard. If you can make it."

" Just drop a ladder over the side and I'll make it, Captain."

There was a photographer too, festooned with cameras and exposure meters like a walking Christmas tree. He nearly missed the Jacob's-ladder, and several hundred pounds' worth of equipment narrowly escaped being immersed in sea-water; but he just managed to hang on and a couple of seamen hauled him up over the bulwark.

Wayne shook hands with Barling. " I'm very glad to see you, Captain. We've been keeping our fingers crossed for you."

" So that you could get your story?" Barling said dryly.

Wayne laughed. He had a long, pointed chin and a wide mouth. His manner was casual but he had shrewd eyes. " It's a great story."

" And you want exclusive rights?"

" To your personal account, Captain."

Barling nodded. " You'd better come to my cabin. There are some financial details I'd like straightened out first. The *Sunday Record* isn't the only paper, you understand?"

" I understand perfectly," Wayne said.

Wilson saw the launch from the bridge of the *India Star*, and it confirmed his worst fears. The police were obviously taking no chances. He saw the two men climb aboard the *Hopeful Enterprise*, and he knew that they had come for him. They might not trouble to board the *India Star*, but they would be on hand in the other ship. There would be no escape.

At times faint hopes had risen in his mind out of the morass of despondency: hopes that perhaps the two policemen in Montreal had not remembered him, had not connected him with the murdered woman in the apartment house; hopes that he might never again hear anything of that terrible business. He even had moments when he succeeded in convincing himself that it had never really happened, that it had been nothing but a horribly vivid nightmare. But those moments soon passed; he knew that it had been real, that he had in fact committed a murder. Yet still there had remained the faint possibility that he might never be suspected, like a small glimmer of light in otherwise complete darkness. Now the glimmer was gone, the last hope destroyed. The police had come. They knew.

The launch had now taken the place of the tug as escort to the *Hopeful Enterprise*; it dawdled along on the starboard beam, holding its speed down to that of the ship. Wayne and the photographer, whose name was Simpson, remained on board the *Hopeful Enterprise*. They moved around the listing, labouring cargo vessel, Wayne asking questions and making notes, Simpson taking photographs. They were like gaudy alien creatures in that setting, with their suède shoes, their Bedford cords and their sheepskin coats. The crew looked at them with interest not unmixed with a certain contempt, but they were all willing to talk and have their photographs taken.

" Front page news, that's us," Lawson said. " Maybe we'll be on the telly."

" With a face like yours, Aussie?" Moir said. " Dinna kid yeself."

There was a feeling of excitement running through the ship. The job was almost done. They had won through.

They had beaten the sea and the tug and they were happy.

Only Trubshaw did not share the excitement or the happiness. He was a sick man; he knew it; he should have been in hospital long ago, and now it might be too late. The pain in his neck, the pain that had moved up into his head and down throughout his entire body, was something more than it should have been if the cut had been healing properly. The thought of gangrene still plagued his mind. When you had gangrene in a limb they amputated the limb, but what could anyone do if it was in the neck?

Tricker had taken the bandages off once or twice, and that had hurt like hell. Tricker had sucked his teeth and shaken his head doubtfully. Trubshaw had asked him what he thought of it, but had got nothing definite. What could you expect from a steward? But that sucking of the teeth and shake of the head were not encouraging; Trubshaw believed that Tricker thought the wound looked bad, even though he did not say as much. And Trubshaw himself knew that it was bad; he could feel that it was. And now perhaps it was too late to do anything about it. Too late.

"Damn them!" he muttered, almost weeping with self-pity. "Damn their rotten 'ides. Lettin' me die."

By nightfall they were nearing land. Barling planned to go in round the south of Ireland and up the Bristol Channel, and he hoped that two more days of steady steaming would see them home. He had spoken to Madden, and the chief engineer had seemed quite cheerful, although it was obvious that he feared to be too frankly optimistic in case that would be tempting fate.

"With luck we may keep them going. I can't guarantee anything, but with luck—"

"Perhaps you'd better slip in a prayer."

" I've been praying for a long while," Madden said; and he did not smile.

From the moment when he had seen the men from the launch go on board the *Hopeful Enterprise* Wilson had been in torment. Where before there had at worst been some tiny spark of hope, now there was none: he would be arrested, he would be tried, he would be found guilty; it was all inevitable. It was not so much the thought of the punishment that appalled him but all the dreadful business that must lead up to it. He cringed at the very idea of standing up in a public court, accused of murdering a woman. How could he bear the shame of it? That would be the real punishment; anything that might come after would be small in comparison.

He could not rest; he had no appetite for food; he roamed about the ship aimlessly, scarcely aware of what he was doing. When he found himself by the hole in the decks amidships he looked down automatically. He could see the water gleaming darkly far below him; it did not appear to have increased much in volume; indeed, the *India Star* had come through her ordeal remarkably well; she was a good sound ship and worth a lot of money, even without the cargo. The underwriters had reason to be pleased.

But Wilson was not thinking of the underwriters; he was seized by an impulse to fling himself down into the hole; it seemed to draw him irresistibly, inviting him. He moved a step nearer to the edge and a broken board gave a little under his weight, almost catching him off balance and throwing him into the pit. With a convulsive effort he managed to pull himself back from the brink, and with a shudder he turned and moved away.

He went back to the cabin, sat down and stared at his hands. It was those hands that had killed the woman. He still found it hard to believe; he could not understand how he had come to do such a thing. He must have been mad. Yes, it must have been that—madness, a fit of madness. But it made no difference; the deed had been done, and for that deed he would be arrested and tried and condemned.

But there was still a way out—one way only; and it was still in his power to take that way, though soon, tomorrow even, it might be denied him. If he were going to take it, he must take it today; this night at the latest. Tomorrow might be too late.

" Oh, God!" he muttered. Oh, God, help me!"

He buried his face in his hands, his whole body shaking.

The moon was shining when he made his way aft. He was carrying a rope coiled over one shoulder and he could hear the water rippling past the ship's side. The sea was calm, and the moon had flung a silver path across its surface, as though presenting an invitation to Wilson to venture out upon it. Wilson had made up his mind: he would accept that invitation.

He reached the stern and took the rope from his shoulder. He made one end of it fast to the taffrail and dropped the other end into the sea. Not hesitating now, he climbed over the taffrail, gripped the rope in both hands and slid down into the water.

After the initial shock of immersion it did not strike him as being particularly cold. He did not let go of the rope at once, but allowed himself to be drawn along in the wake of the ship. He knew that even now it was not too late to change his mind: all he had to do was to climb back up the rope and everything would be as before. He had not yet cut the final link.

He thought about it as the rope dragged him along. Was

he being too hasty? How could he be so certain that the men who had boarded the *Hopeful Enterprise* were in fact policemen? There was no proof of that. But what else could they be? Well, there were plenty of other possibilities: they could have come out on some business connected with the salvage, anything; but just because he had been thinking about the police he had jumped to the conclusion that that was what the men were.

Still clinging to the rope, he turned the matter over in his mind. Suppose the men were not policemen: that would mean that all hope was not yet lost; that there was still a chance that he had not been suspected of having committed the crime, and might never be. For, after all, there was little for the Montreal police to work on; nothing more than a chance encounter with two officers in a patrol car who had probably forgotten him immediately afterwards. It was not as though he had been particularly near the house at that time; he had already walked some distance. The more he thought about it now, the more it seemed to him that he had been worrying without cause. If the Canadians were going to get on to him they would almost certainly have done so before the *Hopeful Enterprise* got clear of the St. Lawrence and would have intercepted the ship in the river. That this had not happened surely proved that he had nothing to fear. He had left it until rather late to reason this out, but fortunately not too late; he had not let go his hold on life.

He decided to climb back on board. It was heavy going; his sodden clothes weighed him down, and his wet, chilled fingers had difficulty in gripping the rather thin rope, which swung from side to side and twisted awkwardly. The ship had a cruiser stern, coming down almost vertically before curving sharply in near water level, and this meant that the upper part of the rope lay close against the hull, making it even more difficult to grasp, especially with the legs and feet.

Wilson was soon gasping with the exertion, and his arms were aching almost unbearably as he inched his way up, slipping back nearly as much as he advanced. But after much effort, and having skinned the knuckles of both hands, he eventually brought his chin level with the deck. He was still clinging to the rope, but the lowest rail was within reach. He let go with his left hand and made a grab at it. The tips of his fingers just touched the rail but could not get a grip on it; and then he began to slide. He made one last despairing snatch at the edge of the deck and felt his nails tear. Then he was falling helplessly, turning over backwards as he fell, so that his head struck the water at the same instant as his feet.

When he came up the stern of the *India Star* was ten yards away, and for all the hope he had of catching it, it might as well have been ten miles. He had lost the ship; he had lost the rope; he had lost his last hold on life.

SIXTEEN

NOTHING TO DO WITH US

CAPTAIN BARLING stood on the bridge of the *Hopeful Enterprise* and watched the grain elevator sucking wheat out of number two hold. He had stood on the bridge in Montreal watching the wheat going in; it seemed a long time ago, the hell of a long time. So much had happened since.

He supposed he should have been feeling happy, or at least satisfied. He had achieved his purpose; he had brought the *India Star* in, and that was what he had set out to do. He had done it for Ann's sake, and for her sake he was glad. But he felt tired and jaded, and there were things that he did not like, things that marred the triumph.

Oh, no doubt it had been fine to steam up the Bristol Channel in his old, listing ship, with people cheering and other ships sounding their whistles, welcoming them like heroes. But he had not felt like a hero, knowing that Able Seaman Trubshaw was lying dead in his bunk, and wondering whether he were responsible for the man's death. For Trubshaw might still have been alive if it had not been for the tow; might even have been alive if he, Barling, had listened to his entreaties, had abandoned the *India Star* and headed straight for home after the tow-rope parted.

Yet Trubshaw had not died from the wound in his neck.

The doctor who examined him said that the cut had been healing perfectly. So why had he died?

There would be a post-mortem and an inquest of course; but none of that would bring Trubshaw back to life. So why had he died? Why? There was something that Orwell, the carpenter, had said, something that had gone round the ship as such things did: " If you ask me, old Trub just died of fear." What had he meant by that? Fear of what? Barling gave it up; it made no sense. All he knew was that, but for the *India Star*, Trubshaw would still have been alive, and that, reason how he might, the seaman's death lay on his conscience like a dead weight.

And Wilson's death too. What had happened to Wilson? There was no clue to his disappearance, unless that rope trailing from the taffrail of the *India Star* could be called a clue. Had the boy fallen overboard by accident or had he committed suicide? But what possible reason could there have been for him to commit suicide? Unless the loneliness had preyed on his mind and driven him out of his wits.

Barling blamed himself for having allowed Wilson to stay on board the *India Star*. He should have insisted that Wilson be taken off; for the boy's own safety he should have ordered Loder to bring him back after the work had been done on the hawser. But he knew that in his heart he had wanted him to remain on board the other ship as a safeguard.

And quite apart from the matter of the chafed hawser, it seemed probable that without Wilson's help he would have lost the prize; for there was a story going round that one night a party of men from the tug had gone on board the *India Star* with the purpose of cutting the tow, and that Wilson had driven them off at the point of a revolver; in fact, had even fired at them, fortunately without apparently hitting anyone. Yet no one had been able to find a revolver on board the ship, though there was some ammunition and a few empty cases lying around. So it looked as if Wilson had taken the revolver with him when he went over-board, though why he should have done that was beyond guessing.

Barling sighed. The financial problem was solved, though it still remained for a court to settle the question of the salvage money. And the irony of it was that Bruce Calthorp would no doubt come in for a share of it as part owner of the *Hopeful Enterprise*. And where was the justice in that? But at least he would get none of the money from the *Sunday Record*; no, not a penny of that. And it was to be a good fat fee, the story having been rendered even more sensational by the two strange deaths and the dark hints of violence. There was mystery too, an unanswered question; and the public liked that kind of thing.

Funnily enough, Calthorp seemed to have had a change of mind and was talking of carrying on with Barling and Calthorp. He had been interviewed on television while the *Hopeful Enterprise* was struggling with her tow in mid-Atlantic, and perhaps he had enjoyed the limelight. It would be right up his street, Barling thought, and of course he would not want to drop out now. Barling did not mind; if Calthorp wished to stay in the firm, that was all to the good; it would avoid a lot of complications. Nevertheless, he felt a certain contempt for a partner who was ready to desert in difficult times but only too willing to stay on when things improved.

He heard a cough, and turning his head saw that the chief engineer had come up on to the bridge. Madden was wearing his shore-going clothes—a baggy, much-worn Harris tweed suit and brogue shoes. He coughed again, somewhat nervously, but said nothing, though it was obvious that he wished to speak.

" Well?" Barling said. " What is it then?"

Madden said with a curious hesitancy: " I was meaning to ask about those engines."

" Yes?"

" You'll be having them seen to?"

" Don't worry about that. We'll get them right before we sail again."

Madden seemed to breathe a shade more easily. " Then you will be—"

" Yes," Barling said. " And I'll want you, Chief."

Madden's head came up. Barling noticed with some embarrassment that there were tears in his eyes. His voice shook a little.

" I did my best."

" No one could have done better."

" Thank you," Madden said. He hesitated, shifting uneasily from one foot to the other. Then: " I'll be getting ashore. I've a phone call to make. To my wife."

" Give her my regards," Barling said.

He ran into Loder some time later. " Well," Loder said, giving his cynical grin, " it all worked out."

" Yes, it all worked out."

Loder said with a touch of hesitancy: " I don't suppose we'll be seeing much more of each other."

" Oh?" Barling said. " What makes you say that?"

" You'll be getting someone else as mate, I imagine."

" Why should I?"

" I think it's been in your mind for some time."

He was right about that of course; it had been in Barling's

mind. But now he was not so sure that he wanted to replace Loder. He still did not like the mate, and probably never would, but he knew that in an emergency Loder was a man he could depend on; and what guarantee was there that a replacement would be as good? Better the devil you knew—

"It's not in my mind now."

Loder looked surprised. "Are you asking me to stay on?"

"I want a chief officer I can trust," Barling said. "I think you fill the bill. That's if you want to sail with me again."

Loder thought it over for a moment, then grinned suddenly without any trace of cynicism. "Since you put it that way," he said, "I'll admit I wasn't particularly keen on looking for another berth."

It was Sandy Moir who found the paper. The steward had used it to wrap some dry stores, and Moir, opening it out, noticed the news item.

"Weel now," he said, "there's a coincidence."

He showed it to Lawson. "Look at that, will ye?"

Lawson looked at it. "So what?"

"D'ye see the date on that paper? It's the day we left Montreal. It's a Montreal paper."

"I can see that. I can read."

"And have ye read what it says there?"

"I've read it," Lawson said. "It says there was a fire in an apartment house. A woman named Roberta Clayton died in it. The fire seems to have been started by a drunk with a cigarette lighter."

"And do ye see where the apartment house was?"

Lawson examined the item again. "Cabot Place."

Moir nodded and looked very knowing. " And where's Cabot Place?"

" In Montreal of course. Where else would it be?"

" Aye, but what part of Montreal?"

" Well, flamin' catfish! How should I know?"

" I know."

" So tell me, chum. Tell me before I die of curiosity."

" That's where we had the set-to with those Swedes," Moir said. " I noticed the name on a wall. That's why I say it's a coincidence. That fire must've happened not so long after. The same night."

" And a woman died in it." Lawson sounded thoughtful. " Wonder what she was like."

" We'll never know."

" No, but it makes you think."

" Aye, it does that."

" Still, it's nothing to do with us."

Moir screwed up the paper and threw it into the garbage can. " No," he said, " it's nothing to do with us."